THE PHONES ARE RINGING FOR *MAIL-ORDER MURDER*

"A charming holiday whodunit. From mistletoe to mayhem, Lucy Stone is an endearing Christmas-time sleuth."
—Dorothy Cannell, author of *The Thin Woman* and *Mum's the Word*

"Some nice plot twists . . . an interesting cast of characters."
—*Publishers Weekly*

"I like Lucy Stone a lot, and so will readers. *Mail-Order Murder* is a delicious slice of Americana, nicely seasoned with mystery. A pleasure."
—Carolyn G. Hart, author of *The Christie Caper*

"Delightful! . . . fine down-home Christmas entertainment . . . spiced with holiday flavor and color throughout."
—*Jackson* (Miss.) *Clarion Ledger*

"An enjoyable read." —*L.A. Life*

"Leslie Meier has succeeded admirably in creating the Christmas ambiance of a small New England town."
—Margot Arnold, author of *The Cape Cod Caper*

Mail-Order
Murder

Mail-Order Murder

Leslie Meier

A Dell Book

Published by
Dell Publishing
a division of
Bantam Doubleday Dell Publishing Group, Inc.
1540 Broadway
New York, New York 10036

This is a work of fiction. Names, characters, places, and incidents either are the product of the author's imagination or are used fictitiously, and any resemblance to actual persons, living or dead, events, or locales is entirely coincidental.

ISBN: 0-440-21452-1

Reprinted by arrangement with Viking

Printed in the United States of America

Published simultaneously in Canada

December 1993

10 9 8 7 6 5 4 3 2 1

*A very big thank you to
Dr. Clifford A. Wood of Bridgewater
State College,
Debi Long, the world's best sister,
and the Twelve O'Clock Scholars*

1

#4076 A set of the most frequently used kitchen knives, including two carving knives, a filleting knife, and a paring knife. All with carbon steel blades and rosewood handles. Our best quality. $57.

"Do you have any really sharp knives?" asked the tremulous voice. "Something that will cut through bone and gristle?"

Lucy Stone stifled a yawn, adjusted her headset, and typed the code for "knives" on the computer keyboard in front of her. Instantly the screen glowed with the eleven varieties of knives sold by Country Cousins, the giant mail-order country store.

"What kind of knives were you thinking of?" Lucy inquired politely. "Hunting knives, fishing knives, pocket knives, kitchen knives . . . ?"

"Kitchen knives, of course," snapped the voice. "Homer hasn't been out of the house for forty years."

Lucy hit the code for "kitchen knives," and the screen listed six sets of kitchen knives.

"I'm sure we have something that will do. How about a set of four carbon steel knives with rosewood handles for fifty-seven dollars?"

"What is carbon steel? Is it really sharp?" insisted the voice.

"Well, some cooks prefer it because it's easy to sharpen. However, it doesn't hold an edge as long as stainless steel. We also have the same set in stainless steel for fifty-seven dollars."

"I don't know which to get. Homer loves to cut and carve. He's really an artist at the dinner table." The voice became confidential. "I've always believed he would have been a gifted surgeon. That unfortunate incident in medical school simply unnerved him."

Lucy stifled the urge to encourage further confidences. "Then carbon steel is probably your best bet," she advised. She then mentioned a related product, a technique her sales manager insisted upon. "You could also get him a sharpening steel. He would probably enjoy using it."

"You mean one of those things you draw the blade against before carving? Seems to me Poppa had one of those. I think you're right; I'm sure Homer would enjoy doing that. It would add a touch of drama. How much are those?"

"We have one with a rosewood handle for eighteen dollars."

"I'll take the knives and the steel."

"All right," said Lucy, smiling with satisfaction. "I need some information from you, and we'll ship them right away." She finished typing in the woman's name, address, and credit card number. "Thank you for your order. Call Country Cousins again, soon." She arched her back, stretched her arms, and checked the clock. Almost ten. Three hours until her shift ended at one A.M.

Lucy didn't mind working at Country Cousins. Like many of the tourists who came to Tinker's Cove in the summer, she was fascinated by the quaint old country store on Main Street. Inside, there were crockery, kitchen utensils, penny candy, and sturdy country clothes as well as fishing, hunting, and camping equipment. The porch with its ten-foot-long deacon's bench, the sloping floors of scuffed, bare wood, and the huge potbellied stove were all authentic, they just weren't the whole story. For the truth was, most of Country Cousins' business came from catalog sales and was conducted at a mammoth steel warehouse on the outskirts of Tinker's Cove. There, state-of-the-art telephone and computer systems enabled hundreds of employees like Lucy to sell, pack, and ship millions of dollars' worth of merchandise twenty-four hours a day, three hundred and sixty-four days a year. Country Cousins was closed on Christmas Day. All merchandise was sold with an unconditional guarantee: "We're not happy unless you are."

"It's quiet tonight, isn't it, Lucy?" said Beverly

Thompson, the grandmotherly woman who had the computer station next to Lucy.

"It sure is. And only ten days until Christmas."

"Are you all ready for Christmas?"

"Not by a long shot," Lucy said. "I haven't finished the fisherman's sweater I'm making for Bill, I still have to make an angel costume for Elizabeth to wear in the church pageant, and I have to bake six dozen cookies for Sue Finch's cookie exchange. And," she continued, "I still have quite a bit of shopping to do. How about you?"

"Oh, I'm pretty well finished. Of course, now that the kids are scattered from Washington to San Francisco there isn't so much to do." Beverly's voice was wistful. "I just have something sent from the catalog."

"Don't knock it," advised Lucy. "I have my mother and Bill's folks coming. Christmas is an awful lot of work. I like Halloween, myself. All you need is a mask and a bag of candy."

"Why don't you all pack up and spend Christmas at Grandma's?" asked Beverly. "I'd love to have my brood back for the holidays." Beverly sighed as she thought of the neat stack of presents waiting in her closet, which she would open all by herself on Christmas morning.

"Oh, we started having Christmas at our house back in the granola years when we had chickens and goats and woodstoves. We couldn't leave or the animals would starve and the pipes would freeze! Now everyone expects it." Lucy shrugged, pausing to take an order for a flannel nightgown.

"I don't know how you girls do it," said Beverly,

picking up the conversation. "You work half the night, and then you take care of your families all day."

"It isn't so bad. I like it a lot better than cashiering at the IGA or working at the bank. When I did that my whole check went for day care."

"But when do you sleep?" asked Beverly, yawning.

"Oh, I usually nap when Sara does. She's only four," answered Lucy, stretching and yawning herself. "It isn't sleep I miss, it's sex. How about you, Ruthie?" Lucy asked the woman on her other side. "Are you getting any lately?"

Ruthie whooped. "Are you kidding? He works all day, I work all night, and the baby wakes up at five." She lowered her voice and spoke in a confidential tone to Lucy and Beverly. "I've asked Santa for a night in a motel."

The three women laughed, and Lucy realized that the thing she liked best about working the night phones at Country Cousins was the companionship and camaraderie of the other women. If you wanted to know what was going on in Tinker's Cove, Country Cousins was the place to be, because absolutely everyone worked there, or had worked there, or knew someone who did. It was an institution; it had been in business for years, selling sporting goods to a small but faithful following of customers. Then fashion seized upon the preppy look, and the demand for Country Cousins' sturdy one hundred percent wool and cotton clothes soared. Preppy was followed by country, and in a

few short years Country Cousins had become a
household word in most American homes.

Country Cousins' phenomenal growth, which
had been the subject of an article in the business
section of the Sunday *New York Times,* would not
have been possible without skilled management.
Founded by a discouraged Maine farmer named
Sam Miller in 1902, Country Cousins was still
owned in 1972 by the Miller family. Fortunately for
them, that was the year Sam Miller III graduated
from Harvard Business School. He was followed,
in 1974, by his brother Tom. Together the two
brothers piloted an expansion program that made
Country Cousins one of the nation's largest mail-
order retailers, although it was still second cousin
to the granddaddy of them all, L.L. Bean.

That had meant growth and change for Tinker's
Cove. Intrigued by the folksy catalog, vacationers
began seeking out the Country Cousins store. Big
old homes became bed-and-breakfast inns, motels
were built, and McDonald's appeared on Route 1.
Soon every available piece of commercially zoned
land had been snapped up and Main Street was
lined with outlet stores: Dansk, Quoddy, Corning,
and even a designer outlet featuring Ralph Lauren
seconds. Tinker's Cove residents enjoyed their
new prosperity, but they also complained about
the busloads of tourists who swarmed all over
town making day-to-day activities difficult, if not
impossible, during July and August. In those
months, then, when the phones fell quiet at Country Cousins, the operators exchanged views on

when was the best time to avoid the crowds at the post office and grocery store.

There was no doubt that life in Tinker's Cove, especially in the summer, required a certain amount of planning. Doc Ryder claimed he had noticed a definite increase in stress-related illness such as ulcers and high blood pressure among his patients. On the whole, however, most people in Tinker's Cove enjoyed their new prosperity, remembering the dark days of the oil embargo when the sardine cannery closed.

"You know," said Lucy, "I'm only a couple of hundred dollars short of making an incentive bonus this month."

"That's terrific," Ruthie said. "What will you do with the extra money?"

"Oh, I don't know," Lucy said slowly, savoring the possibilities. "I think I'll take the whole family out to dinner."

"Don't you want something for yourself?" asked Ruthie.

"Not really. Besides," Lucy said, brightening, "if we eat out, I won't have to cook and clean up!"

There was a sudden burst of activity as calls began coming in and the women were kept busy taking orders. Around eleven-thirty the calls finally slowed down, and Lucy found herself nodding off.

"Gosh, if things don't pick up a little, I'm going to fall asleep." She yawned. "I'll never last until one."

"Why don't you take a break and get a cup of coffee?" Beverly suggested.

"Oh, no. If I have coffee now, I won't be able to

sleep later. Maybe I'll just walk around a bit and get some fresh air. I'll be back in five minutes."

Lucy took off her headset and made her way past the other operators in the phone room, out to the corridor. Walking slowly, stretching her arms and legs as she went, she passed the rest rooms and the break room with its coffee and snack machines. She pushed open the fire door to the outside. It had begun to snow, and the cars in the parking lot were shrouded with one or two inches of soft powder. Lucy took a deep breath of the clean, cold air and watched the flakes falling in the light of the lamps that lit the parking lot. They were large and coming down heavily; the town could get a lot of snow if it kept up all night.

Oh, no, thought Lucy. Not a snow day. A snow day meant that all three children would be home; even the nursery school Sara attended three mornings a week would be closed. She had so much to do to get ready for Christmas that she couldn't afford a snow day.

Lucy sighed and stepped back into the warm building. As the door closed it occurred to her that something wasn't quite right outside. She thought she heard a squawk like a duck quacking. But ducks don't quack at night, especially in December. Perhaps it was a laggard goose making a late migration south, or a dog barking. She opened the door for another look and realized she could hear an engine running. The cars were all mounded with snow, yet the hum of a motor broke the silence. This wasn't right, and if something wasn't right, Lucy had to get to the bottom of it.

Lucy took a wooden coat hanger from the rack near the door, wedged it between the door and the jamb, and went out to investigate. It wasn't very cold, and Lucy was comfortable enough in her jeans and wool sweater. Her high-top Reebok athletics left small prints filled with circles in the fresh snow.

As she drew closer to the row of parked cars, the noise of the humming engine grew louder. It came, she realized, from Sam Miller's BMW. The navy blue sedan with the SAM-I-AM vanity plates was covered with snow just like the other cars. The only difference was that the engine was running and a black rubber hose neatly capped one of the twin exhaust pipes and snaked around the car to the driver's window.

Lucy gasped and tried to pull open the driver's door. It was locked, but she did manage to pull the hose out of the window and then ran back into the building as fast as she could. She arrived in the phone room panting for breath and gesturing frantically with her hands.

"Call the police," she finally managed to say to the group of concerned women who were clustered around her.

In a matter of seconds Beverly had the police station on the line.

"A suicide in the parking lot," she repeated after Lucy. "Lucy Stone found Sam Miller's car running in the parking lot, with a hose pumping exhaust into the driver's window." She paused. "No, we'll stay right here and we won't touch anything."

Lucy collapsed on a chair and someone gave her a cup of sweet tea to sip. "Best thing for a shock," they agreed solemnly.

"Imagine, he had a BMW and a Mercedes," commented one of the girls.

"And an indoor pool," added another.

"Really, the fanciest house in town." They nodded in unison, and then Ruthie ventured to add, "And the fanciest wife."

"Fancy house, fancy wife, fancy cars. It just goes to show," said Beverly, "that fancy isn't everything."

Then they fell silent, listening for the wail of the police cruiser's siren.

2

#4791 These white stoneware mixing bowls with blue bands are perfect in any kitchen. Oven-proof and microwave safe. The set of three includes 1-, 2-, and 3-quart sizes. $29.

Home had never looked so good, thought Lucy as she braked to a stop in the driveway. The familiar shape of the old farmhouse comforted her, and the porch light that Bill had left burning for her was welcoming. The old Regulator in the kitchen read 5:05, too late to make going to bed worthwhile.

While Lucy unbuttoned her coat, Patches, the black-and-white tabby, wove herself around Lucy's legs.

"You don't fool me," said Lucy. "All you want is an early breakfast."

The cat flicked her tail impatiently and meowed.

"Be quiet," Lucy hissed as she filled the coffee-pot. "You'll wake everybody up."

For a moment Lucy considered waking Bill to tell him the news about Sam Miller, but she decided instead to let him sleep. She had been awakened so many times at night by hungry babies that she appreciated the luxury of uninterrupted sleep—and Bill had had his share of sleepless nights with the kids. Besides, he'd be waking up soon, anyway. She switched on the coffeepot and sat down on the rocking chair to watch it drip, smelling its wonderful aroma. She sat and rocked, letting the familiar old-house sounds and scents surround and soothe her.

Lucy loved her kitchen. She loved the old Glen-wood woodstove that burned two and a half cords of wood every winter. She cherished the Hoosier cabinet she'd bought at a flea market and spent an entire summer refinishing. Bill had made the cup-boards himself out of maple, and they had scraped and polished the wooden floor together. She'd sewn the blue-and-white-checked gingham cur-tains herself. This kitchen was really the heart of the house, with its wooden rack for wet mittens, its collection of bowls for the cat, and the big round oak table where the family gathered for meals, Monopoly, and checkers.

If she didn't do something soon, Lucy realized, she would fall asleep sitting up. She poured her-self a cup of coffee and began mixing up some Santa's thumbprint cookies for the cookie ex-change. She was just taking the first sheet out of the oven when Bill, looking rumpled and sleepy, appeared in the doorway.

"What are you doing?" he asked.

"Baking cookies to stay awake," Lucy answered.

"Oh," he said, and headed straight for the bathroom. He returned, poured himself a cup of coffee, and sat down at the table.

"You don't usually bake cookies so early in the morning."

"I know. I didn't get home until five and I decided it wasn't worth going to bed." She paused dramatically. "Oh, Bill! It was awful. Sam Miller committed suicide in the parking lot. I was the one who found him."

"Oh, my God. Was it really bad?" asked Bill, reaching for her hand.

"No, not really. All I saw was the hose going from the exhaust to the window. I couldn't get the door open, and I couldn't see much because of the snow. The police came, and they realized it *was* Sam Miller. He was dead when they got there. Of course, we all had to stay and answer questions even though none of us really saw anything at all. We were all in the phone room."

"Gee, I never would've thought that he'd kill himself. He had so much going for him. Maybe it was all too much—too much responsibility, too much stress," said Bill, drawing on his mug of hot coffee.

"I don't think so," Lucy said. "You and I have stress; someone like Sam Miller goes to Barbados. I don't believe it was suicide."

"Oh, Lucy. Just leave it alone. It's none of your business. Promise me."

"I don't know what you mean," said Lucy, lifting the cookies one by one onto a rack to cool.

"You know perfectly well what I mean. You can't just leave things alone. Well, for your information, there are people called police who investigate these things."

Bill paused to take a swallow of coffee and noticed Lucy's jaw had become set in a certain way he'd come to recognize. "Lucy, don't be like this. I'm just saying I don't think you need to get us involved."

He got up from his chair and stood behind her, slipping his arms around her waist and nuzzling her neck with his bearded chin.

"It's Christmastime. Let's just enjoy the holidays, and the kids. We don't have to get involved with Sam Miller's"—he turned her around and looked straight in her eyes—"unfortunate death." As he put his hand on her chin and tilted her face up to meet his kiss, a high-pitched voice broke the morning stillness.

"Mommy and Daddy alarm. Stop that kissing!"

Seven-year-old Elizabeth squirmed her way between them, demanding, "Elizabeth sandwich! Elizabeth sandwich!"

Bill caught her under her arms and lifted her up between them while Lucy covered her sleep-warmed pink cheeks with kisses. Elizabeth squealed and giggled in delight. Elizabeth's happy cries attracted her little sister, Sara, who wrapped herself around Lucy's legs, and her older brother,

Toby, who leaned against the doorjamb with all the sophistication a ten-year-old could muster and asked, "Are we really having cookies for breakfast?"

It seemed to Lucy as if years had passed before she finally drove Sara to nursery school and returned to the empty house, hoping to catch a few hours of sleep. She had the foresight to turn on the answering machine, but it seemed as if she had barely dropped off when she was awakened by a loud banging and rattling at the back door.

Wrapping her log cabin quilt around her, Lucy staggered down the back stairs and across the kitchen to the door. Through the lace curtain she could see a massive blue shape: Officer Culpepper. Opening the door, she realized there was someone else with Culpepper, a slim, serious man wearing a Harris tweed sport coat under an unbuttoned London Fog raincoat.

"Sorry to wake you up, Lucy. A few questions have come up that we need you to answer. This is State Police Detective Horowitz. May we come in?"

Lucy stepped back, allowing the men to enter, and followed them into the kitchen. Officer Culpepper sat right down at the kitchen table as if he belonged there. Indeed, he had often sat at Lucy's table planning Cub Scout and PTA activities. Detective Horowitz was more self-contained. He took off his coat and folded it carefully, then laid it across the back of one of the chairs. He placed his briefcase on the table just so, opened it, and took out a manila folder. Then he closed it and placed it on the floor next to the chair with his coat. Finally he sat down, drawing his chair up to the table and sitting stiffly with his hands on the folder. Lucy herself had collapsed on the corner chair, leaning her elbows on the table and trying to hold up her head.

"Gee, Lucy, you look beat. Let me make some coffee for you."

"What time is it?" she asked.

"About eleven. Do you have to pick up the kids or something?"

"Not till twelve. I slept longer than I thought."

"Not surprising. You had quite a night." Culpepper slipped three mugs of water into the microwave and pushed the start button.

"The instant coffee's in the cabinet over the sink. Excuse me for a minute."

Looking in the bathroom mirror, Lucy decided she'd rarely looked worse. Quickly she washed her face, brushed her teeth, and ran a comb through her hair. She smoothed a dab of moisturizer under her eyes, straightened her sweat suit, gave herself a quick spritz of Charlie, and returned to the kitchen.

A cup of hot coffee was waiting for her, and she sipped it carefully. Detective Horowitz, she noticed, had opened his folder and was clearly ready to begin.

"Now, Mrs. Stone, about last night. What made you decide to go outside? Wasn't that unusual?"

"Not really. The calls had slowed down, I was feeling sluggish, and I didn't want to drink coffee so close to quitting time. I thought a breath of fresh air might perk me up."

"I see. You weren't drawn outside by any unusual noise or occurrence?"

"Oh, no. In fact, the phone room has no windows. When you're in there you have no idea what's going on outside. Sometimes we'll be completely surprised if a storm has blown up during our shift."

"So it was just a normal night for you. There was nothing out of the ordinary until you discovered the car."

"That's right. When I looked out I knew something was wrong, but I couldn't quite put my finger on it. Then I realized it was the car motor running."

"Was that unusual?"

"Oh, yes."

"You didn't think it might be someone arriving for the next shift or picking up one of the girls?"

"It was too early for that. Besides, when you get out of work at one A.M. nobody picks you up. If you've got car trouble, you just get a ride with one of the other girls."

"I see," said the detective, pursing his lips and making a tiny notation on his yellow legal pad. He had a slight lisp, Lucy noticed, and his upper lip was elongated, rather like a rabbit's. Lucy looked at him closely, thinking what a very serious man he must be. He was such a contrast to Officer Culpepper, who had rolled up his sleeves and was cheerfully washing the breakfast dishes she had left soaking in the sink. Perhaps it was his job that made him serious. A man couldn't investigate sudden death all the time without being affected by it.

Looking around her homey kitchen, Lucy thought how living in Tinker's Cove had insulated her, until now, from the random violence and cruelty that was twentieth-century life. Of course, in the fifteen years she and Bill had lived in Tinker's Cove, things had changed, sometimes drastically. When they'd first moved into the old farmhouse, they had heated entirely with wood, and Lucy, like many others, did all her cooking on the old Glenwood. In those days she often took down the long-handled popcorn popper from its hook on the wall and shook homegrown kernels over the wood fire until they popped. It took a little time, but she never felt rushed in those days. Nowadays she was more likely to put a package of preflavored popcorn in the microwave and zap it. Somehow the long, leisurely afternoons with children and friends had vanished; now Lucy was measuring her life in seconds.

"You didn't see any footprints in the snow, or any sign of disturbance?" insisted the detective.

Lucy shook her head. "No. The snow was clean and unbroken. There were only my footprints."

"According to your account last night, the car was locked. Is that right?"

"Absolutely. Once I saw the hose I tried to open the car door. I couldn't, so I just pulled the hose out of the window and went in to call for help. I don't know what else I could have done."

"Oh, you did the right thing, Lucy," Culpepper interrupted. "It was too late to save him."

"Did you know the deceased personally?" asked the detective.

"Well, everybody in Tinker's Cove knew Sam Miller. I wasn't a close friend, I was never invited to his house or anything. But I certainly knew him to say hello to in the street. Most people did. If you work for Country Cousins, he personally hands you your profit-sharing check, and Country Cousins is the biggest employer around."

"That's right," agreed Culpepper. "Everybody knew him."

"And envied him," Lucy added. "That's what I can't understand. Why did he kill himself?"

The detective and Culpepper exchanged a meaningful glance; finally Culpepper broke the silence.

"There's no harm in telling you, I suppose. It'll be in the paper tomorrow, anyway. Sam Miller didn't kill himself. He had quite a bump on his head. He was unconscious when somebody stuffed him in the car and rigged up the hose. Sam Miller was murdered."

3

#5532 An intricately patterned vest knitted in 100% Shetland wool. Designs include Christmas trees, reindeer, and ice skates. Dry clean or hand wash. Natural color with green and red. Women's sizes: S(6–8), M(10–12), L(14–16), XL(18–20). $58.

Lucy leaned back in Sue Finch's antique rocking chair and took a sip of mulled cider. She inhaled the spicy scent of the potpourri Sue had left simmering in a little copper pot on the woodstove and let out a long breath. After the last few hectic days it was wonderful to relax among friends in Sue's beautifully decorated house.

Christmas was Sue's favorite time of year, and she loved using all the decorations she collected at flea markets and antique shops throughout the year. She had no fewer than three Christmas trees: one in the living room, bedecked with baby's breath and ribbons, which were carefully coordinated to go with the Victorian color scheme; one in the family room, decorated with ornaments her children had made; and one in the kitchen, trimmed with cookie cutters and gingerbread men. A collection of teddy bears was gathered in a hutch, lamp tables held a large and valuable collection of St. Nicks, and a twelve-inch feather tree with tiny German glass ornaments stood on the coffee table. Crocheted and starched snowflakes hung in the windowpanes, and a single candle burned in each window.

Looking around at the rosy-cheeked faces and eyes sparkling in the candlelight, Lucy realized she'd known most of these women for her entire adult life. A few were natives of Tinker's Cove, but most were transplants or "wash ashores" like herself and Bill, idealistic young college graduates who had avoided the rat race and looked for an alternative life-style "back on the land." With their *Mother Earth News* to guide them, they'd chopped wood, planted gardens, and recycled everything.

Through the years she'd attended Lamaze and La Leche League classes with these women. In those days they wore hand-wrought silver earrings in their pierced ears, and they drove ancient pickup trucks or huge Chevy Impalas filled with apple-cheeked and overalled children. Conversations had centered around how to get a baby to sleep through the night or how to keep the cabbage moths away from the kohlrabi.

Now they drove Jeep Cherokees or Dodge Caravans, and the dangling earrings had been replaced with discreet gold buttons or cultured pearls. Their faces were still scrubbed clean morning and night, but Oil of Olay was carefully smoothed under the eyes and just a hint of makeup applied. The long, flowing hair of the seventies had been cut, tinted, and permed. Now they didn't look very different from their mothers.

Their lives, however, were different from their mothers'. They all had jobs, some full-time, but most part-time like Lucy. They helped in their husbands' businesses or answered the phone at Country Cousins, and some weren't above waiting on tables during the summer. "How else can you make a hundred dollars in a few hours?" they'd ask each other as they sunned themselves on the beach. They were the mainstay of the Scouts and the PTA; they were the class mothers. The cookie exchange was an established part of their Christmas season.

Sue Finch had been the hostess for five or six years. It gave her an opportunity to show off her decorations, and it gave her friends a chance to socialize during the busy holiday season. Sue held the number of participants to an even dozen, and each woman brought six dozen of her best Christmas cookies. All the cookies were arranged on a long pine trestle table, and the high point of the evening was a leisurely procession around the table, each woman taking six of each cookie. All went home with the same number of cookies they had brought, but each had a dozen different varieties.

And what varieties! It was a point of honor to bring cookies rich in butter, chocolate, and nuts, cookies that required a bit of fussing. Of course, the cookies were to be taken home and saved for Christmas, so Sue always provided a dessert, too. This year it was an elaborate bûche de Noël, a sponge cake filled with chocolate-flavored whipped cream and decorated with meringue mushrooms and drizzles of chocolate and caramelized sugar.

"I just don't know how you do it, Sue," commented Lucy. "Everything is so lovely."

"Oh, well, I'm not working like you are." Sue shrugged. "Lucy, you look exhausted. Are you doing too much?"

"I don't think so. But I haven't been getting much sleep. The police kept us so late the night Sam Miller died."

"That's right," said Pam Stillings, whose husband, Ted, was editor of the *Pennysaver*. "You actually found Sam, didn't you, Lucy?"

"I did and I wish I hadn't. I may have discovered the body, but I didn't even see him. Everyone asks me about it, but I really don't know anything."

"Were you scared?" asked Pam.

"No, not really. Just kind of sick and let down the way you feel when the adrenaline stops flowing. Of course, I thought it was suicide. I didn't realize he'd been murdered."

"Why would anyone think a man like Sam Miller

would kill himself?" demanded Rachel Goodman. "He had everything, including Marcia."

"If you ask me," Franny Small informed the group, "I think Marcia is the prime suspect."

"The wife usually is," agreed Lucy. "But I can't imagine her being mechanical enough to rig up a hose. She might have gotten her hands dirty."

"She really is a stuck-up little bitch. She thinks an awful lot of herself," commented Rachel, running the side of her fork around her dessert plate and licking it clean with her little pink tongue. "When I invited her to join the Friends of the Tinker's Cove Library, she just turned me down flat. Made me feel as if I were social climbing or something. I was just trying to be friendly," Rachel defended herself.

"They may live here in town, but the Millers have never really been part of the town," Sue said. "I mean, there's a certain distance. You wouldn't just drop by for a cup of coffee and a chat."

Lucy chuckled. "Imagine dropping in on Marcia Miller!"

"Oh, Sid got to know her pretty well," announced Sue. "He's spent quite a lot of time in her bedroom."

"Oh, really?" inquired Lucy. "How did that happen? Why aren't you upset?"

"It wasn't like that," Sue admitted. "He installed a closet system for her."

"Tell us more, Sue," said Lucy. "What did he say when he got home?"

"He said she had a lot of clothes, and"—Sue

stretched the words out, clearly saving the best for last—"they have separate bedrooms."

"Really?" Lucy was incredulous. "Lydia, you're always the first to know about these things. Weren't the Millers happy?"

Lydia smiled. "It's not my fault. Kindergartners tell their teacher everything. They just can't keep secrets. But little Sam seems happy enough. He's a quiet little fellow. Not abnormal. I thought, well, maybe he's just a well-brought-up boy with good manners."

"That's not much help," complained Lucy. "What about your mom, Franny? She always knows everything that's going on."

"You can say that again," agreed Pam indignantly. "I saw her at the IGA and she told me that Jennifer had gotten her first period, and that was before Jennifer even got home from school."

Franny moaned. "It's not as bad as it sounds. She's awfully good friends with the school nurse."

"I dread to think what you've heard about my kids," Lucy worried.

"I don't listen to her," admitted Franny. "I've got my own life to live."

"Don't we all. Too much life, in fact. I'm never going to be ready for Christmas. But I still can't help wondering why someone would kill Sam Miller," Lucy said pensively.

4

#1939 Classic neckties made by McMurray woolen mills, weavers of handsome plaid and solid-color woolens for over 100 years. Made in Canada. Dry clean only. Three lengths: boys, regular, and tall. Be sure to specify size and pattern on order form. $12.

The next morning Lucy made breakfast, kissed Bill good-bye, packed lunches for Elizabeth and Toby, kissed them on their cheeks, and waved them off on the school bus. Then she made the beds, washed the dishes, and swept the kitchen floor. Chores completed, she sat down at the big oak table with a cup of coffee and a pencil and paper to take stock of her Christmas situation.

Only seven days until Christmas. One week. Yesterday she'd finished the sleeves of the sweater she was making for Bill. Now all she had to do was sew the parts together and knit the neckband. The tools she'd ordered from Brookstone had come, and she'd used her Country Cousins discount to buy some other clothes for him. Bill was taken care of. She put a check next to his name.

Next on the list was Bill's father, Bill senior. She had used her Country Cousins discount again and bought him a fly-tying set, which was sure to be a big hit. She put a check next to his name.

Below him on the list was "two moms," hers and Bill's, with a row of question marks next to them. Lucy fought down a rising sense of panic, scratched her head thoughtfully with her pencil, and added another question mark to the row.

This afternoon she would finish Elizabeth's angel costume, really just a sack with armholes made from an old sheet. With her long blond hair, a little tinsel, and wings provided by the church, Elizabeth would look lovely. She put a check next to "angel costume."

Looking over her list of toys for the children, Lucy decided there was no way around it. She had to work tonight, and that only left tomorrow, Saturday, for a final trip to the Tons of Toys store in Portland. She wrote "Sat" next to "toy store" and went on to the next item, "meals." Just then the phone rang. It was Sue Finch.

"Sue, I was just going to call you! I had such a nice time last night, and it's great having all those cookies in the pantry."

"Thanks for coming and bringing those Santa's thumbprints. Everybody loves them. Listen, Lucy, are you going to Sam Miller's funeral?"

"I want to," said Lucy. "I'm sure it's going to be the social event of the year in Tinker's Cove. But I have to do some major Christmas shopping in Portland."

"So come to the funeral with me and we'll zip into Portland afterward. You'll hate yourself if you miss it," coaxed Sue.

"Okay, great," said Lucy. She hung up the receiver and called for Sara to come and put her jacket on.

"Come on, honeybun. We've got to get some groceries."

Lucy enjoyed her little outings with Sara. She had just turned four, and she still loved going to the grocery store, the bank, or the story hour at the library with her mother. Before she knew it, Lucy realized, she'd have another touchy preteen like Toby to cope with.

Sara and Lucy took their time strolling through the aisles at the IGA. They debated the relative merits of Cheerios and Lucky Charms and found a great deal on fabric softener, and Lucy decided that a package of cupcakes wouldn't hurt just this once. When it was time to check out, Lucy saw her friend, Miss Tilley, standing in the checkout line behind Barb Cahoon, who was the mother of three basketball-playing sons and had the grocery order to prove it.

"Miss Tilley, is that heavy cream in your basket? You shouldn't be buying that."

"Nonsense, I've had oatmeal with cream for breakfast every morning since I was a little girl.

Hasn't hurt me a bit. Of course, I'm only eighty-three years old."

"You don't look a day over ninety," teased Lucy.

"Don't get smart with me, young lady," retorted the old woman. "Now tell me . . . about this Sam Miller business. Who do you think killed him?"

"I haven't got the foggiest idea," answered Lucy, tucking a stray clump of hair behind Sara's ear.

"I seem to remember that you love to read mysteries. I used to save the good ones for you at the library." Miss Tilley had been the town librarian until the board of trustees finally gathered the courage to retire her forcibly on her eightieth birthday.

"I don't have time for mysteries these days. In books or in real life." Lucy shrugged. "Everybody's saying Marcia killed him."

Miss Tilley raised an eyebrow. "Why do folks think that?"

"I guess because it's the usual thing. Husbands and wives usually kill each other."

"I wouldn't know," observed Miss Tilley. "I've never been married. I would imagine he was killed by someone who had something to gain by killing him."

"Well, Marcia might have gained a lot. First, she got out of an unhappy marriage. Did you know they had separate bedrooms?" Lucy nodded for emphasis. "And, he probably left her a lot of money. Money, and the freedom to spend it. Sounds like a pretty good motive to me."

"Not necessarily. She received a settlement

when she married, but that's all she got. Sam's money is all tied up in the business."

"That's interesting," said Lucy, remembering that Sam Miller's mother and Miss Tilley were close friends. "Who really runs the business? Is it a family board of directors?"

Miss Tilley laughed. "Old Sam hated family squabbles, and he had plenty of them with his wife's family, as I remember. He left the whole kit and caboodle to the two boys, Sam and Tom."

"That means Sam's brother, Tom, might have quite a lot to gain."

"That nasty Viennese doctor probably had a name for it," said the old woman.

"Sibling rivalry," agreed Lucy. "Sam always did overshadow Tom."

"Now Tom will be able to run Country Cousins any way he sees fit," said Miss Tilley, unloading her basket of groceries onto the conveyor belt. "I wonder if there will be any changes."

"I wonder," said Lucy, shaking off the anxious feeling she got when she thought about going back to work. Chances were, she thought as she watched the girl ring up Miss Tilley's order, that Sam Miller's death had something to do with Country Cousins. After all, that's where his body was found. Maybe it was where his murderer would be found, too.

For the rest of the day Lucy tried not to think about Country Cousins. She was scheduled to work at five, and as the afternoon wore on, she began to feel tense and uneasy.

When the old Regulator in the kitchen read 4:45, she climbed into her little Subaru, feeling exactly the way she had the day she went to the dentist to have her wisdom teeth pulled. As she drove the familiar route, she couldn't help thinking about Sam again. He might have been killed because he saw something he shouldn't have. Nobody in Tinker's Cove talked about it much, but like many coastal communities, the little town had had its share of smugglers and mooncussers.

The *Pennysaver* occasionally reported drug busts made by the Coast Guard, so Lucy knew Tinker's Cove wasn't immune to illegal traffic, but she didn't think she knew anyone who was involved. Country Cousins itself imported goods from all over the world, and Lucy, with her flair for the dramatic, had occasionally wondered if something a little more potent might be coming in along with the Peruvian knitwear and Mexican rugs.

As she parked in her usual spot, she wished it wouldn't get dark quite so early. Anyone could be lurking out there, in the dark beyond the bright lights. They certainly hadn't done much for Sam Miller, and she felt like a sitting duck as she crossed the brightly lit area to the safety of the warehouse.

Walking down the hall, Lucy noticed a group of women clustered around the bulletin board in the break room.

"What's up?" she asked Beverly.

"It's just a memo saying the police are investigating Sam's death and asking everyone to cooperate."

"Oh, no," wailed Lucy. "I don't think I can go through that again."

"I'm sure it's just a formality," Bev reassured her. "I haven't seen any sign of police."

"It feels so creepy coming back here," Lucy confessed. "I didn't want to come."

"The sooner you get back to work the better. Come on, hang up your coat," said Bev in a no-nonsense, motherly tone of voice.

Lucy obeyed, and followed Bev to her desk, where she found a bouquet of supermarket flowers waiting for her.

"Oh, you guys are so nice," she exclaimed.

"We knew it would be hard to come back," said Ruthie. "It's been hard for everyone. We're all scared."

"Lightning doesn't strike in the same place twice," Bev said, settling down at her computer station.

"It does if there's a maniac loose out there," grumbled Ruthie. "What did the police ask you, Lucy?"

"Just what I saw, which wasn't much." Lucy put on her headphone and logged onto the computer. "What did they ask you?"

"They haven't bothered with me," Ruthie complained. "But I heard they were in and out of the office all day. They spent a lot of time with Tom Miller and George Higham."

"I suppose they would," said Lucy, taking a call. She was soon busy taking orders, some from as far away as Alaska and California, and talking to the customers made her forget her anxiety. The lines were busy and she didn't even get to take a breather until ten-thirty. She was just coming out of the rest room and heading for the machines in the break room when she met George Higham, the customer service manager, in the hallway.

"Hi, George," she said, and then, plucking up her courage, she asked, "Have the police made any progress?"

"Not as far as I know. Of course, as the memo requested we're asking everyone to cooperate," replied the little bearded man. He was wearing his usual navy blazer, button-down shirt, gray flannels, and tasseled loafers. Lucy noticed that all his clothes were from the catalog.

"I can't help feeling nervous," admitted Lucy. "You don't think Sam's death had anything to do with the company, do you?"

"Of course not," he snapped, bridling at the suggestion. "Now, isn't it time you got back to work?"

"Well, I'm actually on my dinner break right now. I worked right through my coffee break. I'm supposed to get a half hour for dinner, and a fifteen-minute coffee break."

"You don't need to lecture me about the state labor laws, Lucy," said Higham, his face flushing. Then he caught himself, probably remembering some seminar on employee motivation, and stretched his mouth into something resembling a smile. "I see you're quite close to earning an incentive bonus, Lucy. Keep up the good work."

Lucy watched him as he walked down the corridor to the executive offices; then she went into the break room. She bought a package of cheese crackers and a diet soda from the machines and sat down at the table opposite Bev.

"Sam Miller's only been dead for two days, and already things are going to pot around here."

"What do you mean?" asked Bev.

"With Sam gone, guys like George Higham are going to have more power," Lucy said, ripping open the cellophane package.

"Sam was a nice man to work for," Bev agreed. "He had a smile for everybody, and then he left you alone to do your job."

"Those days are over, Bev. George Higham will be looking over our shoulders and poking into everything. He won't be able to pass up a chance to flex his managerial muscles."

"You're probably right, Lucy. But there's nothing you can do about it. Take a word from a survivor and watch your step. Higham's real friendly with Tom Miller. He's the one to watch these days."

5

#2100 Orthopedically correct back cushion for comfort on long drives. Car manufacturers insist on designing automobile seats that are sheer torture for people with weak or injured backs. These sheepskin-covered forms of flexible, durable poly foam are guaranteed to solve the problem. $57.

As she climbed awkwardly into Sue's big Jeep the next morning, Lucy lamented her friend's knack for looking perfect. Her gray tweed coat and black beret were just right for a Tinker's Cove funeral, where too much black would be considered excessive.

"I thought I'd just put this scarf over my shoulder when we go to Portland," said Sue, pulling a piece of red paisley out of her enormous shoulder bag. "I don't want to look as if I've been to a funeral."

That was just the sort of thing Sue would do, thought Lucy, who was making do with a castoff coat of her mother's. There was no point in being jealous; no matter how hard she tried she would never have Sue's sense of style. Lucy would much rather spend an afternoon reading the latest P. D. James than studying the latest *Vogue.* She loved shopping with Sue, though, because no one had a surer nose for a bargain.

Arriving at the white clapboard church with its tall steeple, they paused for a second and looked up at the weather vane. It was a gilded rooster, and Lucy loved the way it sparkled against the clear blue sky.

Neither woman was surprised at the large turnout. They managed to squeeze their way through the crowd to the balcony, where they found two vacant seats behind the clock. They would have to crane their necks to see, but at least they had seats.

Looking around, they saw that everyone in Tinker's Cove seemed to be there—from the selectmen right on down the social ladder to Sol Smith, the man who owned Sol's Septic Service.

At precisely ten o'clock, a hush fell over the congregation as the Miller family entered. First came Marcia Miller, leaning heavily on the arm of the funeral director. She was swathed in a black veil reminiscent of the one Jackie Kennedy wore at JFK's funeral. Next to her, holding her hand, walked five-year-old Sam IV, looking like a small solemn owl in his tiny blazer and short gray pants. The undertaker indicated the front pew and Marcia entered it, alone except for young Sam. Sue and Lucy exchanged a glance, and Lucy found herself working very hard not to giggle.

Following Marcia was Tom Miller, Sam's younger brother, escorting his mother, Emily. Emily Miller, usually a hale and hearty type, looked very old and frail today. Tom helped her sit down and get settled.

Tom had always been considered something of a mama's boy. He still lived in the big Miller house out on the point with his mother. Lucy had always thought of him as a pale imitation of his brother. He and Sam looked a lot alike, but where Sam had a fine head of glossy black hair, Tom's was light brown and thinning.

Sam had always been a bit of a show-off. He drove the BMW with its SAM-I-AM plates, he had the glamorous wife and the architect-designed house with Palladian windows and an indoor pool. Tom, on the other hand, was often seen at local theater productions with his mother and was known to collect stamps. Lucy had long suspected that he was gay. After all, no one's sex life was nonexistent, and since Tom didn't have a public one, she assumed he must have a hidden one, though she'd never voiced her suspicions. Homosexuality was not an approved life-style in Tinker's Cove.

The next three or four pews behind Tom and Emily Miller were filled with an assortment of more distant Miller relatives and senior executives of Country Cousins. Lucy noticed with satisfaction that George Higham was not included in this group, although she was sure he would have liked to be.

The organist struck a few familiar chords, and the congregation all rose to sing "Rock of Ages." Then they sat and read together the Twenty-third Psalm. A period of silent prayer accompanied by several mournful tones from the organ ensued. Then, formalities completed, Dave Davidson, the minister, rose to deliver the eulogy. Lucy thought he looked awkward and uncomfortable standing before them in the black robe he wore for services. His hands clenched nervously as he grasped the lectern and gazed out at the congregation. He glanced once at Marcia Miller in the front pew and began.

"Sam Miller was a man everyone knew and no one knew. He was not a simple man; his life was a paradox. Sam himself was an enigma."

It seemed to Lucy that a rustling, perhaps even a wave of resistance emanated from the Miller clan, but Marcia sat perfectly still, while Sam IV fidgeted beside her.

"To many of you, Sam was the man who had it all. He owned the biggest store in town, had the biggest house and the biggest bank account. Sam could afford things most of us can't, and many of us envied him.

"You might be surprised to learn that Sam envied you.

"To many of you, Sam was your boss, your employer. He was a good man and a fair man; he was

a good man to work for. It's hard to work for a man
and be his friend, too.

"You might be surprised to learn that Sam
wanted to be your friend.

"Sam Miller knew that the success of his busi-
ness and the prosperity it brought had changed
Tinker's Cove. Sam Miller felt badly about that.
Sam Miller wanted to be your neighbor.

"Sam Miller was a wealthy man, a powerful
man, and a successful businessman. Yet he grew
up here in Tinker's Cove and the values of Tinker's
Cove were his values, too. He believed in family.
He believed in hard work. Let us remember him
as he would have liked to be remembered: as a
neighbor, a friend, a man who was one of us."
Here Davidson paused, looked around the church
at the congregation, and picked up the large Bible
that lay on the lectern before him.

As he stood there, holding the Bible in his up-
raised arm, Lucy thought of the prophets of old, of
unforgiving Cotton Mather and fanatical John
Brown.

"The Bible tells us that we must love our neighbor, and teaches us that it is a sin to kill.

"Sam Miller was murdered. His death was carefully planned—engineered—by one of his fellow
beings. We do not know, yet, who his murderer is."
Here Davidson paused and scanned the congregation, as if he expected the guilty one to leap to his
feet and confess.

"I do not think Sam Miller was killed by one of
you. Sam Miller was a man of our town; indeed, he
embodied all that is best in our town. This evil

person"—and here the minister paused before hissing—"this sinner, must have come from outside our town.

"Every night the evening news tells us of the violence that pervades the cities of our country, of international syndicates dealing in drugs and death, and of political terrorism.

"This is the lesson of Sam Miller's death. We must fight the evil that is overtaking so much of the world, and we must keep our town as a good place to let our love for each other shine as a beacon of light in an ever-darkening world. Amen."

Davidson turned away from the pulpit and almost collapsed onto the ornate, gothic armchair that stood behind the pulpit. He stayed there, leaning on his elbow and covering his face with his hand, while they all sang the final hymn.

When it was over, Marcia sailed serenely out of the church, her veils billowing around her face. No one, of course, could see her expression. Lucy did happen to catch a glimpse of Tom Miller's face as he watched Marcia climb into a large black limousine, and she thought he looked perfectly disgusted.

"What did you think of that?" she asked Sue as they drove down the highway to Portland.

"Well, I was surprised to learn that Sam Miller wanted to be my friend. I would have invited him over for potluck if only I'd known."

Lucy laughed. "Me too. And what was Marcia trying to do? Did you believe that veil?"

"I don't know," said Sue, shaking her head.

"She had to do something. The rumors are terrible."

"I don't see how she could have done it. She always wears such high heels. I couldn't walk in shoes like that, much less kill someone."

"One thing you can be sure of," Sue advised her friend. "If she did kill him, she wore exactly the right outfit." They both laughed. "She could have hired someone to do it."

"Maybe," admitted Lucy. "But I saw them dancing at the profit-sharing dinner, and they looked so nice together. I just can't believe it. I've heard that some people think it was Tom Miller."

"Tom?" Sue's voice rose in disbelief.

"Yeah, an extreme case of sibling rivalry. You don't have kids, Sue. If you did, you'd know how murderous things can get. And Sam really did overshadow Tom. Tom might have been seething inside for years."

"Well, I've never noticed him seething. He seems like such a nice boy." Sue laughed mischievously. "And he takes such good care of his mother."

"You're probably right," conceded Lucy. "Dave Davidson could be on the right track. It must be some maniac from outside town. A prison escapee or something. But I thought those guys always play with their victims first. I don't think a homicidal maniac would choose carbon monoxide."

"You think it was a professional?"

"No, I think it was somebody who was afraid of blood. Somebody who wasn't terribly handy with guns and knives." Lucy paused for a minute, then blurted out, "Somebody like me!" She laughed. "That's what I'd choose, if I were going to murder somebody. No mess, no bother."

The rest of the day passed in a frenzy of spending that Lucy feared might wear the numbers right off her Visa card. At the very least, she hoped the closing date for next month's bill had passed.

After they finished shopping at Tons of Toys and loaded the oversized boxes into the car, Sue insisted on a quick trip to her favorite shop, The Carriage Trade. Lucy went along just to look while Sue tried on dresses, and she noticed a basket of scarves marked fifty percent off.

"Do you think my mother and Bill's mother would like those?" she asked Sue as she pulled two, one blue, one red, from the pile.

"Why not? Those are silk. A scarf like that can really make an outfit."

"Okay, you've sold me. Now, let's get out of here."

"Not so quick, Lucy. Bill asked me to be Santa's little helper. He wants you to pick out an outfit for him to give you for Christmas. How about this Oriental poppy dress?"

"Look at the price! I can't get that!"

"Just try it on," coaxed Sue.

In the dressing room, Lucy grumbled to herself as she struggled out of the too tight black skirt she'd cleverly disguised with an oversize gray sweater. The silky red dress slipped on as if it had been made for her. Lucy shook out her hair and looked at herself in the mirror. Even to her critical eyes the dress was perfect. It slimmed her hips, emphasized her bust, and made her skin glow.

"How are you doing?" asked Sue, shoving the curtain aside. "Oh, Lucy. I can't let you out of this store without that dress."

"I give up," agreed Lucy as she handed the dress over.

As they drove back along the highway to Tinker's Cove, the last rays of weak winter sun disappeared and the sky turned dark. Remembering that they'd skipped lunch, Lucy and Sue made a quick detour through a Burger King drive-in and ordered burgers, fries, and soda.

"I shouldn't be doing this," Lucy said with a moan. "I'll get a zit."

"You've got to live dangerously once in a while," observed Sue, wiping a trace of ketchup off her perfect little chin. "You know, Lucy, I've been thinking. If Sam Miller got killed at Country Cousins, it's probably because somebody there is a murderer. I hope you're careful."

"I don't think I've got anything to worry about," said Lucy. "Why would anybody want to kill me? But I do think Sam got killed because he saw somebody doing something they didn't want him to see. That makes the most sense to me."

"Well, I don't want to scare you. But you *are* the one who found his body. The murderer might be afraid you know more than you do. If I were you, I wouldn't go poking around in any dark corners."

"Don't worry about me. I don't have any opportunities to go snooping around, even if I wanted to."

"You can't fool me, Lucy. I know you too well," said Sue, turning the radio dial to a classic rock station. As they drove along together listening to old John Lennon tunes, Lucy thought how glad she was that she had a friend like Sue. The trip home went quickly as they munched their fries, talked, and sang along with the radio. Soon they had turned off the highway onto Route 1 and had passed through Tinker's Cove center and turned onto Old Red Top Road. Lucy's driveway was just ahead.

As Sue turned into the driveway, the headlights picked out a huddled clump of black-and-white fur.

"Oh, Lucy! Isn't that your cat?"

"It sure looks like it. Probably hit by a car. Stupid cat. I never could teach her to stay out of the road." Lucy began unloading her bags and packages. "I don't know how I'll tell Elizabeth. She loved that cat." She waved to Sue and trudged over to the little furry body. It was definitely Patches.

Lucy took a deep breath and marched toward the house, clutching her Christmas presents and bearing bad news.

6

#7059 Our frosted-glass night light gives a comforting glow as well as a reassuring sense of security. UL tested. $9.

Lucy stashed her packages in the ell off the back door and let herself into the house. She followed the sound of voices into the living room, where she found Bill perched on a stepladder in a tangle of Christmas lights and greenery.

"You're putting the tree up," accused Lucy. "Weren't you going to wait for me?"

"Of course. We were only getting it ready," Bill reassured her as he climbed down. He looked at her closely. "Did shopping tire you out?" he asked sarcastically. "I've got a big pot of clam chowder sitting on the stove, I've spent quality time with my children—a lot of quality time, I might add—

and I'm ready for a beer. Do you want something?"

"A glass of wine?"

Bill went off to the kitchen, and Lucy hugged Sara, who was tugging on her coat and squealing, "What did you get us?"

"Yeah, what about us!" demanded Toby.

"Seven days till Christmas and you're asking for treats?" Lucy raised her eyebrows in disapproval.

"Don't you know that Santa might be watching?" inquired Bill, returning with the drinks.

"Oh, nobody believes that stuff," Toby grumbled.

"Nobody believes in Santa?" Bill was incredulous. "Do you believe in Santa, Elizabeth?"

"Yes, I do." She nodded her head gravely.

"What about you, Sara?"

"I believe in Santa, Daddy."

"Well, I'm glad to hear it. It seems to me that you're in the minority here, my boy." Bill looked sharply at his ten-year-old son. "Perhaps you'd better rethink your position."

Lucy laughed and drew three candy canes from her pocket. "You can chew on these while you mull things over."

The three children happily grabbed the candy canes and went off to watch the *Garfield Christmas Special,* which was playing on the VCR.

Bill and Lucy retreated to the kitchen, where Bill stirred his chowder and Lucy slumped at the table, sipping her wine.

"Patches is out by the road. She must have gotten hit."

"Shit, what a crummy Christmas present."

"I don't know how I'm going to tell the kids."

"Don't look at me," said Bill. "That's your department. I'll handle the graveyard patrol."

"Maybe we can find a little Christmas kitten. They'd like that," said Lucy, sitting up straighter.

Later that evening, after the family had eaten their chowder supper and trimmed the tree, Lucy supervised the Saturday night baths while Bill went out to bury the cat. It was a clear, starry night and not too cold. He picked a spot near the compost heap and began digging. The ground wasn't frozen yet, and his shovel went into the loamy soil easily. As he worked he couldn't help thinking that if an occasional dead cat was the worst thing he and Lucy had to face, they were pretty lucky.

But when he picked up the dead animal to place it in the small grave, he noticed a bit of cord around its neck. He turned on his flashlight in order to get a better look, and he saw that the cat had definitely been strangled with the cord. He dropped the cat into the grave and began shoveling the earth back as quickly as he could. As he replaced the shovel in the toolshed, he tried to think who would do a thing like that. He wondered if Toby had had a fight with someone at school. He couldn't imagine an adult strangling a cat. Not an emotionally healthy one, anyway. Entering the house, he shook off the sense of unease he'd felt outside. From what he could hear, Lucy had her hands full in the bathroom.

She had put both girls in the tub together and

was trying to convince Sara that washing her hair every now and then was really necessary.

"What do you mean we can't stay up and watch the *Peanuts Christmas Special?*" interrupted Elizabeth.

"It's too late. Daddy will tape it and you can watch it tomorrow."

"I want to see it tonight."

"Me too."

"Well, you need your sleep tonight. Tomorrow you're in the Christmas pageant." Lucy's knees were beginning to get sore, and her leg muscles ached from leaning across the tub. "Let's get finished up here."

Toby appeared in the doorway, causing Elizabeth to scream and grab for the shower curtain.

"Relax, Elizabeth. I don't think he's interested in your little pink shrimp body. What's up, Toby?"

"Mom, I can't find Patches. Have you seen her?"

"Actually, I have." Lucy paused, and all three children stared at her, the two girls pink from the hot bath and Toby in his striped pajamas. "Patches got run over," she said slowly, watching their faces carefully for a reaction. "I don't think she even knew what happened. She was a happy cat, right up to the moment she died," Lucy reassured them as she wrapped Sara in a towel and began to dry her. Noticing the tears welling up in Elizabeth's eyes, she said softly, "I'm sure she's in cat heaven right now."

"Patches was the best cat we ever had," Toby asserted. "She used to sleep with me."

"And she'd ride in the doll carriage," added Elizabeth. "Sometimes she'd let me dress her up."

"But then she'd scratch and run away," remembered Sara, ever the realist. "See my scratches." She pointed to two red lines on her forearm.

"She didn't scratch because she was bad," Elizabeth said, defending her pet.

"It's just the way cats are," added Toby. "I didn't mind the scratches. I loved Patches."

"Well, we all loved her and we'll miss her," said Lucy, folding the towels and hanging them up. "Maybe Santa will bring a new kitten."

After she had finally gotten the children tucked in bed and read them the Patches memorial bedtime story, James Herriot's *The Christmas Day Kitten,* Lucy was exhausted. It had been a long day and she was glad to sink into a hot bath herself and let her tense muscles relax. It was an effort to make herself climb out of the tub and get dried off. Then she pulled about ten yards of flannel nightgown over her head, smoothed Oil of Olay under her eyes, and brushed her teeth. On her way to bed she detoured through the living room, where Bill was stretched out on his recliner, flipping through channels with the remote control. She stood next to him and smoothed his hair affectionately.

"I'm going to bed early tonight."

Bill nodded. "Toby having any trouble at school?" he asked.

"Not that I know of. Why?"

"Patches wasn't hit by a car. There was a string around her neck. Somebody strangled her."

Lucy was stricken. "Who'd do a thing like that?"

"Most probably a boy of a certain age."

"You don't mean Toby? He's really upset."

"No, not Toby." He stroked her hand. "Maybe some kid with a grudge against him. Has he said anything?"

"Nope. He seems to get along with everybody." Lucy's voice was defensive.

Bill shrugged. "Don't worry. Go to bed. I'll be up soon."

"That was a nice thing you did today. Thank you." Lucy sat on his lap.

Bill grunted. "What do you mean?"

"You know. Having Sue make me buy an outfit."

"What did you get? Something sexy?"

"No, something beautiful. And expensive. Sue said money was no object."

"I didn't tell her that." Vertical lines appeared on Bill's forehead.

"I can take it back," Lucy said quickly.

"No. I'm just teasing. I like to see you in new things. Are you going to model it for me?"

"You'll see it on Christmas," said Lucy, yawning. "It'll be a surprise."

Bill smiled. "Okay. Go to bed, sleepyhead. I just want to see the end of this hockey game. I'll be up soon."

Once she was tucked under the down comforter in the antique sleigh bed, Lucy realized she wasn't as tired as she'd thought. She reached for the latest Martha Grimes novel she'd pounced on at the library. Soon she was absorbed in the adventures of Detective Inspector Richard Jury and his faithful sidekick, Detective Sergeant Wiggins. What exactly, she wondered, was a Fisherman's Friend?

In the book they came in packets. Perhaps they were cigarettes or a candy of some kind. Maybe a cough drop. She imagined the sharp smell of tobacco and the clean, astringent scent of camphor. When she was at summer camp years ago, she had been terribly homesick. For some reason she couldn't remember, the camp nurse had given her cotton balls soaked in camphor. Remembering the smell made her feel small and sad. Camphor and gray wool army blankets. She'd hated the rough blanket, so unlike the soft blue one on her bed at home. One night she'd kicked off the sheet and become entangled in the coarse gray wool. Somehow she hadn't been able to free herself from the gray wool cocoon and she'd screamed and screamed until the counselor had finally come. The counselor was huge and fat and unfriendly and made her feel small and helpless. The counselor had laughed at her and Lucy had perversely held on to the wool blanket. In her dream she had wanted to be free of it; now she held on to it for protection. Now she smelled the sooty, chemical smell of an automobile's exhaust. It was a comforting, familiar smell and she wanted to yield to it, to the great throbbing sensation of the automobile motor, but she knew she mustn't. She must fight to stay awake. She felt warm fur on her face as if the cat had curled up to sleep there. The cat began purring softly and then louder and louder until it sounded like one of Bill's power saws. Lucy's heart began beating faster and faster; it was pounding within her chest and she couldn't breathe. Her lungs were bursting and she finally fought her way free of the suffocating covers. Gasping and gulping for air, she realized she was sitting up in bed. Her nightgown was soaked with sweat and she was shaking with fright. She put her hand to her forehead to push her hair back and realized that her hair was soaking wet. It must have been a nightmare; there was nothing to be afraid of. Bill was lying there beside her, sound asleep. She took a deep breath and tried consciously to relax her arms and legs the way she had learned in Lamaze class. She really ought to get up and go to the bathroom if she wanted to be comfortable, but she was afraid to leave the safety of Bill's side. The thought of walking alone through the dark, silent house terrified her. Instead she turned on her side and curled against him, spoon fashion, to try to go back to sleep.

7

*#9997S   Traditional Christmas wreaths made by
skilled craftswomen from genuine Maine balsam.
Each wreath is decorated with a weatherproof red
bow. $16.*

"Mommy, isn't that wreath big?"

Lucy smiled down at Sara, who was dressed in
her prettiest Polly Flinders dress and was sitting
beside her in the crowded church pew.

"Yes, it's very big," agreed Lucy as she admired
the enormous green wreath that hung behind the
pulpit. Lovingly assembled by the flower committee, the wreath was the only decoration in the
plain   Protestant   meeting   house.   Sunlight
streamed through the tall windows and reflected
off the white walls. This church had no stained
glass or carved-wood paneling; there was no kneel-
ing, no sense of hushed anticipation. Members of

the congregation greeted each other and chatted while children ran up and down the aisles. This was the Sunday of the Christmas pageant, and the church was overflowing with families. A chord from the organ brought everyone to order, and the congregation rose to sing an old carol, "Venite Adoramus."

Lucy loved the pageant. It was the same every year, and she enjoyed watching the children progress through the ranks. The very youngest were angels, naturally angelic with their plump rosy cheeks and soft baby hair, but they soon graduated to become sheep and other animals. After a year or two the animals went on to become shepherds. The very oldest had the important parts: Mary, Joseph, the Three Wise Men, Herod the King, and the angel Gabriel. This year Elizabeth was a lead angel and Toby was a shepherd. Little Sara was still too young, so she was watching with her parents and dreaming of next year, when it would be her turn.

Lucy had grown up in New York City, where her family had attended a large and wealthy Episcopalian church. As a child she had taken part in the Christmas pageant there, dressed in elaborate costumes donated by a rich parishioner. That pageant had been a very elaborate affair, complete with hired actors and singers for the main parts. It had been wonderful in its way; the darkened church had smelled of evergreens and the candle-lit, glittering processions had been dramatic and mysterious. Yet Lucy much preferred the sunlit, homemade pageant in Tinker's Cove.

Hearing the familiar strains of "Angels We Have Heard on High," Lucy craned her neck to see Elizabeth. She nudged Bill and they beamed with pride as their daughter, glowing with self-consciousness, paraded down the aisle. This year she even had a line. Lucy perched anxiously on the edge of the pew until Elizabeth announced, "Behold, I bring you tidings of great joy!" and she could safely relax.

Leaning against the straight back of the pew, Lucy thought how different the atmosphere in the church seemed today from yesterday. Yesterday's mourners had been replaced with families intent on celebrating Christmas. It was wonderful to see so many young families in the church, thought Lucy. When she had first started attending, Toby had been a baby and she had come to services with him cradled against her chest in a Snugli.

The congregation then had consisted mainly of old people; some Sundays the youngest member was sixty-seven years old! The women in particular had made Lucy feel welcome. They had fussed over baby Toby, delivered casseroles to her house when she caught pneumonia, and given her slips and cuttings from their gardens. Lucy was truly fond of some of the old members like Miss Tilley. She smiled to see her gaunt figure and straight back across the aisle.

When Miss Tilley had been the librarian at the Broadbrooks Free Library, she had been legendary for her strict overdue book policy and her tart tongue. She was not likable, but she had a penetrating intelligence that earned her the town's re-

spect. It was rumored that she had been friends
with Longfellow's daughter, Alice, and Lucy always meant to ask her if it was true.

Next to Miss Tilley sat Faith Willets. Faith was a
simple, good-hearted woman who dressed in plain
old polyester from Sears—and had the most beautiful garden Lucy had ever seen. Faith was the
president of the Organic Gardening Club, and
wrote the "Garden Checklist" that appeared in
the *Pennysaver* each week. The acre surrounding
her Cape Cod house was planted like an English
cottage garden with fruit trees, perennial flowers,
herbs, and even vegetables. Faith was the primary
donor to the Memorial Day plant sale, and Lucy
was a faithful customer.

In fact, Lucy had first discovered the Tinker's
Cove church through the annual plant and used-
book sales. One year Bill had discovered a treasure trove of erotica in the paperback section and
had returned hopefully every year since. When she
felt lonely and depressed after Toby's birth, Lucy
began attending services. She'd given up trying to
be an Episcopalian in her teens when she'd decided she just couldn't believe in God. She'd
missed the hymns and sermons, however, and had
been delighted to discover the friendly, informal
community church. Shortly after she'd become a
member, old Dr. Greenhut died and the congregation called a new, young minister, Dave Davidson.

Dave and his wife, Carol, were not a traditional
ministerial couple. Carol avoided the Women's
Club meetings like the plague and rarely attended
Sunday services. Instead she poured her energy

into her career as a sculptor and turned the old barn behind the rectory into a studio. The congregation didn't seem to mind; in fact, the Davidsons brought a new energy and vitality to the old church. Sunday school classes were organized and filled rapidly as many young families realized something was missing from their lives that church could provide.

The service was ending. Everyone rose to sing the "Hallelujah" chorus from Handel's *Messiah.* No one could resist joining in, and the church was filled with the sound of joyous if somewhat off-key voices raised in celebration.

Lucy left Bill in the line of parishioners waiting to greet the minister and, taking Sara with her, went to find Toby and Elizabeth. Truth be told, she always felt awkward around large male authority figures like Dave and could never think of anything to say to him.

Back home and changed out of their Sunday best into jeans, Lucy and Bill made lunch and planned the rest of the day. Since the weather was so beautiful, they decided to take turns staying with the kids and going out for a run. Once the dishes were washed, Lucy put on her sweat pants and running shoes and headed out alone along the network of dirt roads that crisscrossed the woods. They were originally made by early settlers who cut timber for firewood, but nowadays they also led to hunting and fishing camps. They were ideal for a peaceful jog when the weather was warm; once the ground was covered with snow they were perfect for cross-country skiing. Today Lucy stood for a while on the back porch, taking a few deep breaths and deciding which route to take. Because she hadn't been running much lately, she decided on an easy four-mile loop without hills that went around Erskine's Pond. She did her stretches and set out, enjoying the bright sunshine and mild weather. The last few winters had followed a pattern of mild weather until Christmas; then once the holidays were over, bitter cold and heavy snow storms set in. It seemed as if this year was going to be no exception.

Once she got past the mile mark—an old Chevy truck that someone had left to rust in the woods—Lucy found her stride. The first mile was always the hardest, but she'd learned that if she didn't give up, the rest was easy. She felt as if she could run forever along these soft roads, smelling the sharp, piny scent of the trees and catching glimpses of the pond sparkling through the trees. Problems and anxieties receded, leaving nothing but the pounding of her heart, the rhythmic in and out of her breath, and the regular thud of her feet on the path. All too soon she saw the tall, narrow chimney of their house, and rounding the bend, she saw Bill and the kids in the yard. Bill and Toby were tossing a football back and forth, and the girls were mixing up pine cone and stone soup. Lucy cooled down by walking around the house and then went in for a drink of water and a shower. As she closed the door she saw Bill wave as he started off on his run.

* * *

Since Bill was a more enthusiastic runner than she was, Lucy didn't expect him back for a while. After her shower she settled down to stitch together the pieces of the sweater she had knitted for him. The girls were happy in their room playing with their Barbie dolls and Toby curled up in a corner of the couch with his book report book. It was only when she noticed the light getting dim and reached to switch on the lamp that she realized how late it was. According to the old Regulator, it was almost four, which meant that Bill had been gone for nearly three hours.

Lucy tried to fight her rising sense of panic. Something must be wrong; he could have—indeed he had—run the Boston marathon in that time. She didn't think he would have attempted anything so ambitious today. He knew she had to leave at five to pick up her mother at the airport.

Something must have happened to him, she thought. But what? He was a big strong man in his prime. Of course, Sam Miller had been in his prime, too, and someone had managed to kill him. She knew she was being ridiculous. No one wanted to kill Bill. But when she switched on the porch light and stood looking out the door, she couldn't help remembering Patches' lifeless body lying in the driveway. It was getting too dark to wait any longer, she decided. She would have to take out the Subaru and look for him. She piled the kids into the car and slowly and carefully drove along the rutted, twisted dirt road. Running along these roads was one thing; it was quite another to drive them at night, even in a four-wheel-drive. The woods were gloomy, filled with dark, shadowy shapes, and the branches brushed and snapped against the car.

Lucy gripped the steering wheel in clenched hands, her neck and shoulders rigid with anxiety as she searched for him. When she finally saw his familiar figure in the road, the tension drained from her body, leaving her with a terrific headache and aching muscles.

Bill was moving slowly, however, and as he came closer, Lucy could see he was limping.

"What happened?" she asked as he climbed into the car.

"I must have pulled a muscle or something. God, my knee hurts."

"Do you need a doctor?"

"No, I'll put some ice on it when I get home. How late is it? Don't you have to get to the airport?"

Lucy checked her watch. "It's almost five. I'll drop you at the house and get the kids something to eat on the way. McDonald's okay, kids?"

As Lucy sat on the molded plastic seat in the airport, she knew she had made a mistake. Having grown up on a steady diet of tofu and brown rice, the kids adored McDonald's. Their excitement, fueled by excessive amounts of sugar, caffeine, and saturated fats, was almost unbearable. Her mother's plane was due at seven o'clock, and Lucy very much hoped it would be on time. She could see her reflection in the expanse of plate glass that overlooked the runway. She was a very small figure, surrounded by a moving blur of brightly clad children.

"Please sit down and wait nicely for Grandma," she begged through clenched teeth.

"Ooh, here comes another one!" shouted Toby. The girls screamed and jumped from their seats, running to press their hands and noses against the window.

"Is it Grandma? Is it Grandma?" they demanded.

Lucy checked her watch. Five minutes past seven. "Maybe," she said. "I hope so." Actually, she rationalized, this isn't so bad. At least she wouldn't have to face her mother alone. Ever since her father had died six months ago, Lucy had dreaded being alone with her mother. When she last saw her mother, the pain of her loss was so palpable that Lucy could barely stand to be with her. One look at her grief-ravaged face and Lucy had wanted to flee back to the safety of Bill's arms, back to the cocoon of her house. "There is no safety, no security," her mother's reproachful eyes always seemed to say. "I thought there was, but I was wrong."

Lucy crossed her arms across her chest, pressed her lips together, and looked up to see the automatic doors opening. Her mother picked her way carefully along the rubber matting, holding herself together only by the tightly wound threads of restraint and good breeding. She might well have been the survivor of some dreadful battle or holocaust, a witness to unspeakable horror, scarcely sure herself whether she was alive or dead.

8

*#8990   This canvas-and-leather bag is accepted
by airlines as carry-on luggage and can be neatly
stowed under the seat. Seasoned travelers advise
that one's necessities should not be entrusted to
the airlines, as they can be lost or delayed. Sturdy
webbing shoulder strap included. 16″ × 12″ × 10″.
$89.*

"Hi, Mom," said Lucy, rising from her seat and
brushing her cheek against her mother's.

"Hello, Lucy," her mother responded tone-
lessly.

The children gathered around her, waiting ex-
pectantly to be fussed over, but their grandmother
didn't seem to notice them.

"How was the flight?" Lucy asked, searching
her purse for change to give the kids so they could
buy gumballs from the machine.

"It was fine," her mother answered automatically.

"Well, do you have a baggage check or anything? How do we get your bags?"

"A baggage check?" Her mother seemed never to have heard of such a thing.

"Didn't you hand over your luggage at the ticket counter?" Lucy demanded.

"I guess I must have. I don't have it now."

"No, you don't," agreed Lucy, fighting the urge to take her by her shoulders and shake her. "You must have checked your bags, and they gave you a ticket. Do you remember what you did with it?"

"No, I don't," admitted her mother. "I don't remember that at all."

"Well," said Lucy, speaking softly and patiently as she might to one of the children, "how about looking in your pockets and your purse. I don't think that man will let you take a suitcase without your ticket stub." She indicated an extremely large uniformed baggage attendant.

The older woman obediently went through her pockets and found nothing, so Lucy led her over to the row of seats so she could sit down and search her purse.

"It isn't here," her mother announced.

"What is that pink paper?" asked Lucy, spying a corner peeking out of an inner zipped compartment.

"I don't know," she replied, and pulled out a stub printed with large black numbers. She sat and looked at the paper, turning it over and over.

When she made no effort to move, Lucy said, "That looks like it. Let's give it a try, okay?"

"All right," her mother agreed, following her over to the baggage carousel.

"What does the bag look like?" asked Lucy. "How many are there?"

"Just one."

"Do you see it?" asked Lucy.

"No, I don't recognize any of these."

Lucy bent over and began comparing the strips attached to the bags with the stub in her hand. She soon found a bag with matching numbers and asked, "Is this it?"

"It could be." She was open to the possibility.

Lucy picked up the bag. "Now, where did the kids go?"

"The kids?"

"You know. My children. Your grandchildren," snapped Lucy, her patience exhausted. "They were here a minute ago."

"They were?"

"Here they are," said Lucy as the three kids ran up. She was almost hysterical with tension and relief, and her head was pounding. "We've got the kids and we've got your bag, I guess we're all set."

"Did you bring us presents?" Toby asked boldly.

"No. I haven't shopped yet." All three children's faces fell with disappointment, but their grandmother ignored their crestfallen expressions and turned to Lucy. "I didn't want to carry the presents on the plane. I thought you and I could go shopping together this week."

"I'm sure we can," Lucy answered in a cheerful

voice, but inwardly she was furious with her mother. One week until Christmas and her mother had just assumed she would have time to take her shopping. Somehow they would have to fit it in, but Lucy already felt deluged with Christmas preparations.

"I'll carry the suitcase, Mom. You take Sara's hand. I don't want her running around in the parking lot. Elizabeth, Toby, stay with me and watch out for cars, okay?"

Lucy had the sudden feeling that now instead of having three children, she had four. She was going to have to take care of her mother as well as her children. The realization absolutely overwhelmed her.

As she led her little cortege out of the terminal, Lucy noticed a taxi pulling up. She was surprised to see Marcia Miller and little Sam IV climbing out of the backseat. As she loaded her mother's suitcase into the Subaru and waited for the kids to pile in, she watched the cab driver unload suitcase after suitcase. Lucy couldn't help but notice that these were not the canvas bags sold in the Country Cousins catalog; these bore the distinctive gold logo of Louis Vuitton. A long trip to someplace warm, thought Lucy as she put the key in the ignition. Not a bad idea at all. She wondered if she could stow away on their flight.

Arriving home, Lucy installed her mother on a corner of the couch, switched on the TV for her, and sent Bill in to keep her company.

"How's the knee?" she asked as he hobbled past her.

"The ice helped, but it still hurts. If it's not better tomorrow, I'll go and see the doctor."

Lucy sighed and went upstairs to get the kids ready for bed. Toby and Elizabeth could change into pajamas themselves, but Sara needed help. It was way past her bedtime, and she burst into tears when Lucy told her it was too late for a story. Bending down to kiss her good night, Lucy noticed that her forehead was awfully warm. A quick check with the thermometer revealed a temperature of a hundred and one. As Lucy counted out the cherry-flavored tablets, she wondered idly what else could go wrong this week.

That night she ran her bath as hot as she could stand and in a fit of self-indulgence poured in the last of her treasured Vitabath. As she leaned back in the delicious suds, she sighed and felt tears prick her eyes.

This was going to be an awful Christmas. It had been terrible to lose her father just a few months earlier. He had died suddenly of a heart attack. He had left for work as usual one morning, and by dinnertime he was lying in the intensive care unit of the hospital.

Lucy had rushed to her mother's side and supported her through the hurried hallway conversations with doctors, who held out no hope, through long visits during which her father gave no sign he knew them, and she helped her make the difficult decision to forgo heroic measures and let nature take its course. Then there were the funeral and cemetery to arrange, accommodations to find for out-of-town relatives, and food to prepare for all of them.

After two weeks in the city Lucy was exhausted. She needed to go home. She helped her mother find an accountant to help put her affairs in order and then she left, feeling tremendously guilty but knowing that her place was in Maine. She called once or twice a week and made the occasional brief visit, but even though her mother had seemed awfully depressed over the phone, it had still been a shock to find her so passive and out of touch at the airport.

She had to face the fact that the mother who had been a friend and confidante was gone. Lucy promised herself that she was not going to worry about taking her shopping. If the weather was too bad, or if there was no time, she could just tie a twenty-dollar bill to a candy cane for each of the kids. Feeling somewhat relieved, Lucy was again flooded with depression when she remembered that Bill's parents would be arriving on Friday. Christmas seemed like a huge snowball increasing in size as it rolled downhill. She was a small figure in its path, toiling up a mountain of baking, shopping, and wrapping.

She was reluctantly pulling herself out of the water when Bill appeared in the bathroom.

"Now, there's a sight for any man," he said, grinning and handing her a towel.

"Oh," she groaned, "I'm getting so fat."

"No, you're not," he said, drying her back. "You're just right. There's something the matter with your mom, though. She keeps talking about things that happened years ago. She's mad at Aunt Beverly for borrowing a pair of stockings sometime during World War Two. Beverly just took them without permission and got a run in them."

"Doesn't surprise me. Just the sort of thing Aunt Beverly would do." Lucy nodded.

"Aunt Beverly? She's a sweet old thing who weighs about ninety pounds!" exclaimed Bill.

Lucy laughed. "You didn't know her in her prime. I think she borrowed a boyfriend along with the stockings. I know what you mean about her state of mind. It's not good. Maybe after she's been here for a few days she'll get better. I hope so. I don't know what I'm going to do if she doesn't."

9

*#3221 Hand-knitted ski hat worked in 100%
llama wool by Peruvian natives. These unique
hats are attractive and warm. In shades of brown,
taupe, and natural. One size fits all. $39.*

At a few minutes before five the next afternoon,
Lucy pulled into the employees' parking lot at
Country Cousins. She sat for a few minutes, waiting for a song on the radio to finish, and smiled
wryly to herself. For the next few hours all she had
to do was answer the customers' calls and press a
few buttons on her computer keyboard.

"You need a pair of waterproof boots? We have
just the thing. What size do you need? Where shall
I ship it? What is your credit card number?" The
next day the boots would be on their way. If the
boots were out of stock, Lucy would know immediately, thanks to the computerized inventory sys-

tem that Sam Miller had pioneered. The computer would suggest an alternative style and indicate when the next shipment of boots would arrive.

Out-of-stocks were unusual at Country Cousins because Sam Miller had also developed a computer program that tracked the ebb and flow of customer preferences in the past and projected future sales. Lucy had come to develop a real respect for the computer, which always greeted her personally when she logged on. The screen would blink a friendly "Good evening, Lucy!" after she logged on with her password, Patches.

"You look beat," Beverly said sympathetically. "Christmas getting to you?"

"Sort of," agreed Lucy, taking a call for a decorative maple sap bucket. Calls came in pretty steadily for about an hour, and the time flew by as she placed orders for a chopping block, a fishing rod, a camp stove, and lots of deerskin slippers. There was a lull around six, dinner hour, and the evening was slow.

"Except for a few last-minute orders for slippers, it seems as if everybody's got their shopping done," Beverly observed.

"I've sold quite a few slippers, too." Lucy laughed. "You'll never guess who I saw at the airport," she said, pausing for emphasis. "Marcia Miller and little Sam and a big pile of suitcases. It looked as if she were planning to be away for a while."

"I guess the police don't think she's a suspect, then."

"Do they really say that?" came Ruthie's voice

from the computer station on Lucy's other side. "Don't leave town, ma'am," she said, mimicking Jack Webb on *Dragnet*. "I don't think they can. Unless they indict you, I think you can go wherever you want."

"It kind of makes her look guilty, leaving like that so soon after the murder," Beverly commented.

"How could a woman kill a man after she'd had his child?" asked Karen Hall, pausing on one of her frequent trips to the rest room. She rubbed her huge tummy absentmindedly. "It just doesn't make sense to me."

"I know," agreed Lucy. "But they say that the spouse is always the first suspect. She didn't have to do it herself. She might have had a boyfriend, or even hired somebody. She certainly could have afforded to."

"But why? Why would she kill him?" questioned Ruthie. "He seemed nice enough. And she had everything she could want. That nice little Mercedes, that big house, all those clothes."

"Money's not everything," said Beverly, shaking her head.

"They had separate bedrooms. For all we know, she could have hated him." Lucy broke off the conversation, nodding her head toward the end of the row of work stations, where George Higham had suddenly appeared.

Karen scuttled off and the rest of the women bent their heads over their desks in an effort to look busy. Lucy hoped he would pass by, or that someone would call with an order, but the indicator on her phone refused to light up. She hunched over her desk and began making a tally of the items she had sold that night.

"Lucy, how are things going?" As George stopped behind her he blocked the overhead light and a shadow fell over her tally sheet.

"Just fine, George. I've been selling a lot of slippers."

"Keep up the good work," he said, letting his fingers linger as he patted her on the shoulder. Then he moved along down the row.

Lucy stood right up and marched off to the rest room. She resented George touching her, and even though she washed her face with cold water, her cheeks remained flushed with anger.

Back at her station she muttered to Bev, "I think somebody ought to check up on George's whereabouts last Wednesday night."

"Just because he's obnoxious doesn't make him a murderer," Bev cautioned her.

"Everyone knows how ambitious he is. And Sam Miller never gave him the time of day. Maybe he figures his chances are a lot better with Tom Miller," Lucy said darkly.

"Speak of the devil," whispered Bev. Lucy looked up and saw George and Tom Miller standing together by the door to the phone room. Tom cleared his throat rather loudly, and George rapped on a file cabinet to get the women's attention.

"I just want to let you know that we're having a problem here," said Tom in his high-pitched voice. He paused and the women shifted on their seats, waiting nervously.

"We have a mouse in the house." He smiled apologetically. "A few field mice have apparently moved into the building." A few of the women giggled.

"This is a serious problem for us," he continued. "They could damage the computer. We've discussed the options, and I've decided the most humane course of action is to trap them."

He held up a small wire-mesh box.

"This is a Havahart trap. We don't want to hurt them, we just want to catch them and release them out in the woods where they belong. I just wanted you to know how we're dealing with this. Any questions?" He waited, glancing around the room.

"We want to make one thing very clear," added George. "It is company policy to allow eating only in the break room. If any of you are discovered with food in your desks, I can assure you that you will be dealt with severely." He turned and ushered the senior executive out of the room.

"Better clean out your desk, Karen." Lucy giggled, watching as Karen pulled out wads of crumpled candy wrappers.

"It's just that I get so hungry," Karen confessed. "I'm hungry all the time."

"I know. Being pregnant is the one time you can eat without feeling guilty," Lucy reassured her. She continued thoughtfully, "I guess we can eliminate Tom Miller as a suspect."

"I didn't know he was," observed Bev.

"I heard he was," Ruthie agreed, giggling. "Who knows what evil lurks behind that mild-mannered exterior?"

"I don't think a man who uses a Havahart trap to catch mice is going to murder his brother," said Lucy. "Dave Davidson is probably right. Sam Miller must have been involved in something outside Tinker's Cove, something illegal like drugs."

"Smuggling cocaine in the Peruvian ski hats?" asked Ruthie.

"Oh, I don't know," Lucy admitted. "It's hard to believe Sam would be involved in anything like that."

"That's it!" exclaimed Karen. "They wanted him to smuggle in dope and when he refused they killed him."

"I think you better answer your phone," observed Bev.

"Oops! Country Cousins. May I help you?" Karen babbled automatically. When she finished taking the customer's order, Lucy heard her muttering.

"What's the matter?"

"I'm out of order forms."

"I'll get 'em for you," offered Lucy. "They're kind of heavy."

"Thanks," said Karen. "I'll cover on your computer."

Lucy went over to the corner of the big phone room where the boxes of computer order forms were kept, but she discovered that the usual supply of boxes was gone. She would have to go to the storeroom.

She hesitated. The storeroom was down a long, dimly lit hallway. The furnace room was along there, and the maintenance department. But no one would be there now; the offices would be dark and empty.

Before Sam Miller's death she'd never given her safety a thought at Country Cousins. But now she was reluctant to leave the brightly lit phone room and the safety of the group of chattering women.

Straightening her shoulders, she pushed open the door and marched down the hallway, away from the phone room. She turned right where the hallway branched into the executive suite and the maintenance offices. The door to the storeroom was unlocked, and she pushed it open, reaching for the switch.

She was relieved to see several pallets of paper neatly stacked near the door and hurried in to pull a box from the top. Juggling the heavy cardboard box, she turned to leave when she saw George's figure in the doorway.

"What are you doing in here, Lucy? You're not supposed to leave the phone room."

"I just came to get order forms," explained Lucy. "There were none in the corner where they usually are."

"You should have notified your supervisor," George admonished her.

"I didn't want to waste the time, George. Now, can I get by? I want to get back to work."

"Let me carry that, Lucy. It must be heavy."

As George took the box of paper, his fingers brushed against her breasts. "You know, in many ways you're a model employee. And you're very pretty, too." George's voice had become hoarse.

"Thank you." Lucy smiled at him sweetly. "You know, George, my husband is six feet tall, and he pounds nails all day long. If I told him that you touched me, he'd beat you to a pulp. He would." She nodded. "Shall we go back to the phone room?"

"I guess you can manage this box after all," said George, thrusting it at her. His face was very red, and there were beads of perspiration on his brow. Lucy hurried off. But inwardly she shuddered, unable to forget the sickening feeling of George Higham's clammy hands on her sweater.

Back at the safety of her desk, Lucy was suddenly exhausted. She answered the phone mechanically and couldn't help keeping an eye on the clock. The calls dribbled in, and the clock seemed stuck at twelve-thirty. Finally, at one, it was time to go home.

As they were putting on their hats and coats, Ruthie looked over her shoulder uneasily. "I'll tell you one thing," she said. "I hope they catch whoever killed Sam Miller real soon. It feels creepy around here."

"Ladies, don't forget your paychecks." George stood by the door with a handful of envelopes. Country Cousins had always followed the old Maine custom of paying on Monday. That way, the paternalistic mill owners had reasoned, the workers wouldn't drink away their earnings over the weekend.

Lucy snatched her check from George, refusing

to look at him. Before she left the building, she made sure that her car keys were ready in her hand. She went straight to her car, scanning the parking lot to make sure no attacker was lurking. She unlocked her car door quickly, made sure no one was hiding in the backseat, and climbed in, locking the door immediately. It was only after she was safely in her car that she noticed the other women clustered together by the door. She started the car and circled around the lot to the group, rolling down her window.

"What's the matter?" she asked.

"I've been laid off," announced Bev, her voice flat with shock.

"Me too," Karen said with a moan.

Lucy ripped open her envelope immediately, but only her check was inside. She still had a job, but she wasn't sure she wanted it.

10

#4152   These heavy-duty coffee mugs are favorites with merchant seamen and railway crews. They are extremely sturdy and keep coffee hot for a long time. $8.

"It's a crime, I'm telling you, a crime." Officer Culpepper's voice boomed over the din in Jake's Doughnut Shop. Jake's was everybody's favorite coffee shop, and today, four days before Christmas, it was packed. Lucy didn't go to Jake's very often; somehow her days didn't include time to dawdle over coffee, and even if she had the time, she didn't want to be tempted by the doughnuts.

But at noon Bill had come home early and announced that his knee was bothering him and he was going to take the afternoon off. Sara was feeling much better, so Lucy decided to seize the opportunity and take her mother shopping. They had gone through most of the stores in town, and everywhere they went her mother had the same comment.

"I just don't see anything here that I want to buy," she would say, shaking her head and clutching her purse with two hands.

Lucy couldn't decide if she really found all the shops uninspiring or if she just couldn't bring herself to part with any money. Lucy knew her mother had been well provided for, but she suspected that the loss of her father's weekly paycheck had made her nervous about spending anything at all. Passing Jake's, Lucy had seen an empty table and suggested they stop for coffee. She needed a break, and her mother could certainly use the calories.

"I've heard those Bavarian cream doughnuts are delicious. Wouldn't you like to try one?" she urged her mother.

"Oh, I never snack."

"You've been losing weight. You should have a snack now and then," said Lucy, forcing herself to make eye contact with her mother. She hated to see her dull eyes, sagging cheeks, and lank hair.

"Oh, I eat very well. I eat three meals every day."

"Well, it's obviously not enough. You must have lost twenty pounds since Daddy died."

"It isn't because I don't eat enough," she insisted. "I do."

"That can't be true. You're using up more calories than you're taking in. If you want to stop losing, you're going to have to eat more. Have a doughnut."

"Just coffee, please," her mother told the waitress.

"Me too," said Lucy, resigned to losing another round. Looking around the shop, she saw her friend Lydia Volpe, the kindergarten teacher, just coming through the door.

"Hi!" She waved, and Lydia headed over, cheeks cherry-red from the cold.

"What a day! Those kids have got too much Christmas spirit!"

"I can imagine. Lydia, this is my mother, Helen Hayes."

"I'm not the actress," Lucy's mother announced.

"No, I can see that. I mean, you don't look at all like her," said Lydia. "It must be confusing sometimes to have the same name as a famous person."

"Usually I use my husband's name, Mrs. Bernard Hayes, if I'm reserving a hotel room or ordering something over the phone. I started doing that because once when I went to Washington, D.C.—it was during the war and I was visiting my sister who was stationed there. Well, I reserved a room at the Hilton because it was the only hotel that had any vacancies. I just gave my name, Helen Hayes, but when I got there they took me up to an enormous suite. It was just beautiful and was filled with fresh flowers. They thought I was the actress."

As she listened to this story for the hundredth time, Lucy thought how bright and animated her mother had become. It was as if her real life had been some time in the past, and the present was

just a pale imitation, which she didn't find very
interesting.

"What did you do?" asked Lydia. "Did you stay
in the suite?"

"Of course not. I couldn't have afforded it. But it
was lovely, and they let me take one of the flower
arrangements to my new single room, courtesy of
the management. They wanted to thank me for being so cooperative."

She nodded virtuously, certain in the knowledge
that she was not one to make a scene, and sipped
her coffee.

"What's Culpepper so het up about, Lydia?"
asked Lucy. "He's been ranting and raving since
we came in."

"Probably the warrant for the special town meeting. Haven't you seen it?"

"No, I've been a little out of touch lately," said
Lucy, glancing at her mother.

"Everybody at school was talking about it. It
calls for a one-year moratorium on all building,
and sets aside most of the undeveloped land in
town as conservation land. Sam Miller had been
working on it before he died. It's kind of his legacy
to the town."

"No wonder Culpepper's upset," commented
Lucy. "First the layoffs and now this. There won't
be any jobs left in town."

"I heard about that. Are you okay?"

"So far." Lucy shrugged, watching as Barney
Culpepper grabbed a young man wearing a ragg
sweater by the shoulders and shook him.

"Who's that?" asked Lucy.

"Jonathan Franke, the new APTC director," answered Lydia. "Association for the Preservation of Tinker's Cove," she added for Helen's benefit.

Conversation in the coffee shop had stopped. Everyone watched to see if there would be a fight, but Culpepper merely dropped his hands and mumbled something to Franke, who left.

"It's just not fair," the officer said to his companions. "People in this town care more about osprey and owls than they do about people. I've worked here my whole life, but I can't afford to buy a house. In fact, my rent's going up next month and I don't know how I'm going to pay *that*."

His companions nodded and murmured assent.

"Now they want to stop building houses for a year. What's that going to do to you, Mark?"

"I'll have to go someplace else, I guess. Especially since Patti got laid off last night. I sure as hell ain't gonna make it here."

"I'm thinking of switching to remodeling," admitted Frank Martignetti, a master builder known for his expensive custom homes.

"Good luck," said Culpepper. "You'll have a devil of a time getting anything approved by that planning commission. Nope, this town is a good place to live if you're an owl or a salmon, but it really stinks if you're a workingman." He set his police cap squarely on his head, shifted his holster, and stalked out the door.

"Gosh, I hope nobody's double-parked out there," Lucy quipped.

"He has a point, Lucy. It's very hard for young

people to get a start here," said Lydia. "Most of my students' parents are really struggling."

Lucy nodded. "The average house costs about a hundred and fifty thousand dollars."

"Right," said Lydia. "Say he makes twenty-five thousand, and she makes twelve, that's thirty-seven thousand a year. Most people don't even make that; a lot of our kids get subsidized lunches. But, say a family is doing pretty well, they're both working, they still can't afford twelve hundred a month for a mortgage payment—and that's if they've managed to get together thirty thousand for a down payment."

"We're lucky we bought when we did."

"We are, too. But you know there was talk of affordable housing for town employees like cops and teachers. Not that I like being considered a town employee lumped in with the road crew and the water department." Lydia's dark eyes flashed. "I'm a professional with a master's degree. But it would have helped some of the younger teachers. If this plan is passed by town meeting, I don't know what will happen to that."

"I didn't realize Sam Miller was behind all this. Maybe that's what Dave Davidson was talking about in his sermon. It didn't make sense to me," Lucy confessed.

"Maybe. Maybe it was just something Marcia put him up to saying. Socking it to the family that Sam didn't want to be like them, he just wanted to be one of the folks. She hated the Millers. You know what else I heard?" Lydia's eyes grew large and she dropped her voice. "I heard she had an affair with Culpepper."

"No." Lucy giggled. "With Culpepper? The woman who brought Donna Karan dresses to Tinker's Cove?"

"And sculptured nails!" Lydia laughed.

"And black eyeliner!"

"Don't forget black stockings." The two women burst out laughing.

Noticing that her mother had withdrawn from the conversation and was just sitting at the table fingering her napkin, Lucy reached over and caressed her hand.

"What do you say we make a quick trip to Portland? There's a big toy store there."

"I don't want to buy them toys." Helen shook her head. "They have too many toys already."

Lucy tapped her fingers on the table. "We've been to every store in town, and you didn't find anything. What do you have in mind?"

"I don't know. I'll know it when I see it," she said, frowning.

Lucy rolled her eyes and looked at Lydia, who asked, "Have you been to Sandcastles?"

"What's that?"

"A little shop behind the fire station. It's cute. She does T-shirts and sweat suits. She'll monogram them or put designs on, whatever you want."

"There wouldn't be time now to have something monogrammed," Helen argued.

"Oh, sure there is. She can probably do it while you wait."

"Let's check it out, Mom. Thanks, Lydia. See you later."

Just as Lydia had promised, Sandcastles was located on pilings behind the fire station. As they walked along the boardwalk the cold wind from the bay whipped their clothes and faces. Lucy took her mother's arm and guided her along protectively, afraid the wind would be too much for her. Once inside the little shop filled with brightly colored clothes, they began to warm up.

Energized by Jake's coffee, Lucy convinced her mother to buy each of the girls a sweat suit printed with dancing hippos. While they waited the proprietor applied rhinestones in strategic places, a detail Lucy knew would thrill Sara and Elizabeth. For Toby they found a warm sweat shirt with a surf design.

"Lucy," complained her mother, "I didn't really plan to spend this much."

"The kids will love them. How much did you have in mind? I'll make up the rest."

"You don't need to do that. I'll manage." She sighed.

"Good."

"I'm not made of money, you know."

"And you're not the actress, either," said Lucy, piloting her mother back along the boardwalk to the car. "Christmas only comes once a year. Let's try to enjoy it, okay?"

"I'm trying," answered the older woman.

"I know you are," Lucy said, and as the wind whipped round them in a savage burst, she felt tears sting her eyes.

11

*#1009   This rugged compass is an essential sur-
vival tool that no hiker should be without. Sturdy
plastic case with a leather strap. $11.*

Waking up the next morning, Lucy experienced
an almost paralyzing sense of dread. She knew
with certainty that something awful was going to
happen today but couldn't remember what. She
checked the calendar, but no dentist appoint-
ments were penciled in and she hadn't forgotten
anyone's birthday, but she knew that there was
something unpleasant in the offing. When the
phone rang promptly at eight, it all came clear.

"Lucy, this is Marge Culpepper."

"Hi, Marge."

"Listen, Lucy. I can't help you with the Cub
Scouts this afternoon. I've got to take my mother
to the doctor."

"Cub Scouts?"

"Don't tell me you've forgotten? You and I promised to fill in for Kathy—she's leaving today to spend Christmas with her family in Pennsylvania."

"I did forget. I haven't got anything planned."

"Well, you've got until two-thirty to think of something. I wish I could help you, but Mom's feeling pretty poorly. You know, it's a nice day and not too cold. Why not take them for a hike?"

"That's a good idea. They can work off some of their excess energy."

"Sure. And I'll send my husband over with some hot cocoa. It's the least I can do. He'll be at Indian Rock at, say, three-fifteen. Okay?"

"Sounds great. Thanks, Marge."

Lucy hung up the phone and started washing the breakfast dishes. At least now she knew why she was depressed. Cub Scouts always depressed her.

Of course, Toby loved being a Cub Scout. He loved wearing his blue-and-gold uniform to the after-school meetings every Wednesday. He was doggedly working his way through the wolf book, bringing it to her to sign after he finished each task and proudly supervising the addition to his uniform of each bead and patch that he earned. Toby was the ideal scout, and Lucy felt guilty that she couldn't be the ideal den mother.

She did help out from time to time, and when she did she always took two aspirins before the meeting. No matter how much time she spent planning activities and projects, it never took the boys more than five or ten minutes to lose interest. Then came the choruses of "We're bored" and "What's next?" As far as Lucy could tell, all the boys really wanted to do was wrestle with each other and pick on Stubby Phipps, who, they all agreed, was a nerd. Oh, well, she sighed, maybe today would be different.

Leaving her mother in charge of Sara and Elizabeth, Lucy was waiting in the elementary school cafeteria at two-thirty for den five to assemble.

"Where are we going today?" asked the boys.

"We're going to hike up to Indian Rock," she announced enthusiastically.

"A hike. . . ."

"I'm too tired."

"We'll never make it, it's too far." They groaned in protest.

"You sound more like Girl Scouts than Cub Scouts," Lucy teased.

"But what about a snack?" demanded Stubby. "Aren't we going to have a snack?"

"No snack!" Den five was dismayed.

"I've heard a rumor that an old Indian, the last of the Sockatumee tribe, may have left a peace offering at Indian Rock."

"What? What tribe?"

"Haven't you heard of the Sockatumees?" Lucy asked incredulously. "Don't you know their secret word?"

"What secret word?" Toby was suspicious.

"I'll teach it to you. Repeat after me. Oh!"

"Oh."

"Oh-wa." Lucy waited.

"Oh-wa," repeated the boys reluctantly.

"Oh-wa-ta," said Lucy, drawing out each syllable.

"Oh-wa-ta," the boys intoned.

"Oh-wa-ta-foo." Lucy smiled.

"Oh-wa-ta-foo," repeated the boys.

"Oh-wa-ta-foo-lie." Lucy restrained the urge to giggle and kept her voice low, stretching each syllable out as long as she could.

The boys repeated after her, "Oh-wa-ta-foo-lie," really beginning to get in the spirit of magic Indian words.

"Oh-wa-ta-foo-lie-yam," droned Lucy, and the boys shouted back:

"Oh-wa-ta-foo-lie-yam!"

Lucy beamed at them. "Now, say it faster."

"Oh, what a fool I am!" they screamed.

"Gotcha!" said Lucy.

"You tricked us," Toby reproached her.

"I didn't spend five summers at Camp Wah-wah-tay-see for nothing," Lucy confided, leading the boys out the door and across the baseball field, where the trail to Indian Rock began. "Now, let's see who'll be the first to reach Indian Rock."

"Last one there is a rotten egg," shouted Eddie Culpepper, and the boys ran ahead along the trail, except for Stubby. Stubby was a little overweight, and he was content to walk along beside her.

"Mrs. Stone, did you really spend five summers at camp?"

"I did."

"My mom wants me to go to camp this summer." Stubby didn't sound very happy about the idea.

"Don't you want to go?"

"Nah."

"Why not?"

"I don't like sports much," Stubby confessed. "I like to read. The Three Investigators are my favorites."

"Toby likes them, too. There'll probably be time to read at camp. I used to read Nancy Drew books. Lots of the girls had them, and we'd borrow the ones we hadn't read."

"Yeah? I still don't think I'll like it."

"You might be surprised." Lucy smiled. "We'd better catch up with the others." She had been keeping track of the boys' progress by listening to their voices, but she hadn't heard them for a while.

When they rounded the last bend in the trail she was relieved to see the seven other members of den five perched on the huge boulder.

"Stubby Phipps, Stubby Phipps," Rickie Goldman chanted. "It ought to be Chubby Hips, Chubby Hips."

"That's enough, Rickie," reproved Lucy. "Who knows the story of Indian Rock?" She was wondering where Officer Culpepper and the hot chocolate were.

"It was left here by a glacier," Stubby said. "Mr. Hutchins told us about it."

"That's true," agreed Lucy, who knew better than to dispute anything a teacher said. "But I was thinking of the Indian legend. Does anybody know that?''

The boys were quiet, so she began.

"The story goes that a long time ago there was an Indian chief named Maushop. Maushop was a great chief, and his people loved and respected him. His tribe was very rich and they had lots of corn in their storehouses, and deerskins and wampum. But even though he was very rich, Maushop's greatest treasure was his little son, Queeg. Maushop loved watching Queeg play and grow. Maushop taught him to fish and hunt and track, and Queeg grew up to be the best hunter in the whole tribe.

"But then a sickness came and many people died. It was a hard time for the tribe, and there was a great deal of suffering. The people came to Maushop and said that since he was the chief he should do something.

"So Maushop climbed up the hill where we're standing and called to the Great Spirit.

"The Great Spirit answered, but he demanded that Maushop give him something that was dear to him.

"So Maushop went home, wondering what he could offer to the Great Spirit. He looked at his favorite bow and arrows, the moccasins his wife had sewn for him, even his best knife. While he was doing this Queeg entered the lodge, and Maushop knew what was dearest to him. So he told Queeg to go to the top of the hill.

"Queeg climbed the hill, just like you did today. Maushop followed behind him, and when Queeg got to the top he called out to the Great Spirit. 'Great Spirit, here is my offering, my dearest son.' Then a great eagle came out of the sky and swooped down, grabbing Queeg in his enormous talons and carrying him off.

"Maushop stood there, all alone, crying for his son. The Great Spirit spoke to him. 'Because of your great sacrifice the people will live and prosper. To remind them of your great sacrifice, I will put a mark here so they will remember Queeg and how you loved him very much, but you loved your people even more.' Then the eagle came flapping out of the sky, holding this rock in his talons. He dropped it here, and it's been here ever since."

The boys were quiet, looking thoughtfully at the rock and glancing at the sky.

"I don't believe it," Eddie announced.

"Me neither," agreed Rickie.

"But it was a good story, Mrs. Stone," Stubby reassured her.

A sudden squawk made them all jump, and Lucy looked up. Officer Culpepper was pulling into the parking lot in his police cruiser. He climbed out of the black-and-white car and walked over to the group, carrying a large Thermos and a bag of doughnuts.

"You boys ready for some hot cocoa?"

Rickie had already opened the bag and the boys were pushing and shoving, grabbing for the doughnuts.

"Hey," he thundered. "That isn't how scouts

behave. Get in line. Take turns. There's enough for everybody."

"That's amazing," commented Lucy as the boys obeyed. "I'd give anything for a voice like yours."

"Well, Bill probably wouldn't like it very much."

"No. I don't think he would." Lucy laughed. "It would make being a den leader a lot easier, though."

"I s'pose," agreed Culpepper, taking an enormous bite of doughnut.

"Any new developments in the Sam Miller case?" asked Lucy. "Have they found out who did it yet?"

"Not that I know," Culpepper said. "Of course, I'm just a town cop. They don't tell us much. We're just supposed to direct traffic and find lost bicycles and leave the investigating to the state police." He shrugged. "Last year the town wouldn't even give us a cost-of-living increase. Nobody thinks much of us."

"These scouts certainly think you're something special," said Lucy, indicating the boys, who were admiring the officer's uniform and cruiser.

"Is that a real gun?" asked one of the boys.

"It sure is. It's a police-issue nine-millimeter Smith and Wesson," he answered, drawing the revolver from its holster. Lucy eyed the gun distrustfully. "Don't worry, Lucy. I made sure the safety's on."

Culpepper held the gun out in the flat of his hand for the boys to admire, then twirled it around his finger a few times before replacing it at his side.

"What else have I got in my belt? This here's my walkie-talkie. We use this when we're working in a team—say, for the Fourth of July parade or a search. A situation like that." He held up the instrument for the boys to see and then stowed it in his belt.

"I tell you, this belt gets heavy. At the end of the day I'm sure glad to take it off. Now these," he said, "these are handcuffs. Who'll volunteer?"

All the boys stuck out their hands, but Culpepper picked his son, Eddie, and clapped the cuffs on him. "Now, see if you can get loose," he challenged. The boys gave Eddie all sorts of advice, but no matter how he twisted and turned the cuffs held fast.

"Okay, I'll unlock him. I've got the key right here."

A sudden burst of sound from the radio in the cruiser caught Culpepper's attention as he unlocked the cuffs. "I have to answer that. Want to see how the radio works?"

The boys all followed him over to the black-and-white vehicle. Lucy remained leaning against Indian Rock, overwhelmed by a sudden sense of recognition. She'd heard that sound before. But when? Not in the course of daily life; she'd heard it in connection with something major. How else could she explain the uneasy feeling that threatened to overwhelm her? She followed the boys over to the cruiser and tried to remember if she'd seen a police cruiser at her father's funeral. Death. She knew the sound meant death.

This is ridiculous, she thought to herself, and then she remembered. She'd been standing in the doorway at Country Cousins watching the snow fall. She'd stepped inside and closed the door. Then, she'd heard a sound. Because of the sound she'd gone out and found Sam Miller. And it wasn't a dog barking, she now realized with horror. It had been the crackle of a police radio. She was sure. That meant a police cruiser had been in the Country Cousins lot when Sam Miller was dying. Had it been Culpepper's?

As Lucy watched him pushing buttons and talking into the mike, smiling and nodding at the scouts, bits of information fell into place. It was rumored that Culpepper had had an affair with Marcia Miller. Even if that wasn't true, Miller's role in the planning commission might have been enough of a motive. Just yesterday at the coffee shop she'd seen him nearly sock Jonathan Franke over the commission's proposal. He had certainly looked as if he'd wanted to kill Franke.

"That's enough, boys," said Culpepper, looking up at Lucy. He looked away furtively, and she realized he knew that something was wrong.

"Boys!" she called. "It's getting late. It's time to go back." They had run off down the trail without her. She half turned toward Culpepper, stretching her lips across her dry teeth in something she hoped looked like a smile.

"Thanks so much for bringing the cocoa," she said. "I'd better catch up with the boys."

"Not so fast," said Culpepper, causing her to

stop in her tracks. She stood nervously while he hauled himself out of the cruiser, calculating her chances. She was perhaps twenty feet from the cruiser. If she ran immediately, she would have a good head start. She was used to running, and a glance at Culpepper's belly where the buttons on his uniform strained to hold the gaping fabric together indicated that he wasn't. If she ran hell for leather down the path this instant, she could catch up to the boys and be safe. But she felt frozen in place; her feet felt like lead and her breath was coming too fast. She watched as he came closer and closer, fascinated by the red veins on his nose, the hairs that sprouted between his eyebrows, and his little blue eyes. Piggy eyes. Had Sam Miller felt like this before he died?

"Lucy, breathe into this bag." Culpepper shoved the doughnut bag against her face and picked up her hands, cupping them so she could hold it herself. "You're hyperventilating. Here, sit in the cruiser for a minute until you feel better. Just take it easy. You'll be fine," he reassured her.

"I don't know what's the matter with me," Lucy admitted as he climbed in beside her. "For a minute there I thought you killed Sam Miller."

Culpepper looked up sharply, and again panic swept over Lucy. Why couldn't she keep her suspicions to herself, at least until she was safe at home?

"I know you didn't," Lucy reassured him. "But everyone's saying you had an affair with Marcia Miller."

"What?" Culpepper was incredulous. "Me and Marcia Miller? That stuck-up bitch?"

Lucy shrugged. "You know the kinds of things people say. I thought it was possible."

"You did?" Culpepper sucked in his gut and straightened his shoulders. "Do you think Marge knows?" Then he corrected himself. "I mean, do you think anybody said anything to Marge?"

"No, they wouldn't." Lucy shook her head. People gossiped according to the rules in Tinker's Cove. They talked about each other, but they never made direct accusations.

"And then I saw you and Jonathan Franke in the coffee shop. You looked as if you wanted to strangle him."

"Those conservationists make me sick," Culpepper confessed. "Not a one of 'em knows what it's like to work for a living."

"But Barney . . ." Lucy weighed her words carefully. "I'm almost positive I heard a police radio the night I found Sam Miller. In fact, I know I did."

Culpepper dropped his head on the steering wheel. "I was afraid you'd remember. I tell you, I was sweating like a pig that day Horowitz had me come along to interview you. Boy, was I glad when you didn't remember. I guess it'll all come out now," he said, raising his head and looking at Lucy.

"What will come out? What were you doing in the parking lot?"

"I was a fool," said Culpepper. "I can't believe I was so stupid."

"You're really in trouble, aren't you?"

"You know it. If this gets out, I'll lose my job." Culpepper shook his head. "It's not much of a job, but it's all I've got."

"It can't be that bad," Lucy reassured him. "What did you do?"

"I don't know what I was thinking of," Culpepper admitted. "You know that magazine? *Modern Mercenary*? Well, I've had a subscription for years. Real man stuff, y'know. Lots of action. I love it. In the back they have a classified section. Dirty deeds done dirt cheap, y'know what I mean?"

"I think I saw something on TV about it."

"Yeah, I think *Sixty Minutes* did a story on it. Well, I put an ad in. Partly it was just for kicks, just make-believe. But partly I thought something might come from it. The pay for this job is lousy, and we could use some extra money. So I put an ad in."

His eyes glowed with pride as he remembered the words. " 'Resourceful, enterprising man of action available for assignments in Maine, Massachusetts, and New Hampshire.' I didn't want to be away from home overnight, you know." He cocked an eyebrow and nodded at Lucy.

"Barney, why don't you drive while we talk? When the boys' parents come to pick them up, they'll wonder if I'm not there."

"Okay." He started the car and headed down the road.

"I only got one response to the ad, but it was a doozy. Someone wanted me to kill Sam Miller. Offered me ten thousand dollars. I said I wouldn't do it, wasn't really my line, and they hung right up."

"Who do you think it was? Was it a man or a woman?"

"It was a man, but I don't have any idea who. I didn't recognize the voice and there wasn't time to trace the call. Then I didn't know what to do. If I warned Sam, I'd have to explain about the ad, and I was embarrassed. I might even have lost my job —moonlighting's against the regulations. So I just tried to keep an eye on him. Checked in on him every so often. That night I happened to see him on the road, heading toward the warehouse. Then I got a call to go to the Anchor Bar and give Bill Maloney a ride home. When I got back to the parking lot, Sam was already dead. I didn't have any reason to be in the parking lot, so I left."

"You'd really get in trouble if this got out?"

Culpepper nodded. "Probably get suspended without pay for a month, something like that. I can't afford that." He shook his head and then smiled. "Don't look so worried, Lucy. I'll think of something." He indicated the anxious row of mothers peering into the cruiser and laughed. "I guess I'm not the only one with some explainin' to do."

"I didn't feel well," said Lucy to the small group of curious women. "Officer Culpepper gave me a ride down from Indian Rock."

"These children have been unsupervised for at least fifteen minutes," said Mrs. Phipps, the wattles under her chin shaking with indignation.

"I'm sorry. It couldn't be avoided." Lucy

shrugged. Seeing their skeptical expressions, she didn't think she'd convinced them.

"Don't forget," she added brightly, "there's no meeting next week because of school vacation. C'mon, Toby, let's go home."

12

#6775 This genuine wool blanket woven by MacMurray Weavers of Canada is an authentic reproduction of the blankets the Hudson Bay Company traded for furs. The lines on the side of the blanket indicate how many skins it was worth. White with red, yellow, and green stripes. Specify twin, $95; double, $135; or queen, $175.

"I'm seriously thinking of committing suicide."

"Don't you think you're overreacting just a tiny bit?" Sue's crisp, rational voice came over the phone wire.

"Probably," admitted Lucy. "But you should've seen the way they looked at me. I thought Stubby Phipps's mother was going to lose her bridge. She just kept standing there with her mouth hanging open, looking at Culpepper and looking at me and trying to make one plus one equal something illicit."

"Well, I wouldn't worry about her. If Stubby manages to graduate from high school, he'll be the first in that family."

"But she's influential. People listen to what she says, and she always has a lot to say. I bet the phone wires are just buzzing, and meanwhile my reputation is going down the tubes."

"What if Bill finds out?"

"Sue! There's nothing for Bill to find out! I'm not attracted to Barney at all."

"A lot of women are."

"I have trouble believing that."

"Why? These things happen, you know."

"Culpepper's belly hangs over his pants."

"Just because you don't find him attractive doesn't mean that other women don't."

"Well, I do know Barney. He's a family man, he likes kids, he's kind of an overgrown kid himself. And even if he wasn't devoted to Marge, where would he carry on an affair?"

"There's lots of camps out in the woods. A roaring fire, a Hudson Bay blanket, a man with a gun . . . it could be kind of exciting."

"Whatever turns you on," said Lucy, neatly turning the tables on her friend. "Seriously, it's an awful feeling when you know people are talking about you. I feel so exposed. I can understand how Marcia Miller must have felt. No wonder she left."

"That, or a guilty conscience?"

"Who knows?" said Lucy, growing impatient. "Look, I've got to go."

She hung up the phone and turned to see her mother entering the kitchen. She was glad to see she was still in her robe and slippers. So far during her visit she had appeared fully dressed each morning. When Lucy went in to tidy Toby's room she found both twin beds neatly made and her mother's suitcase zipped shut and placed at the foot of the bed.

"Did you have a good night?" asked Lucy.

"I did," answered her mother, pouring a cup of coffee. "I've slept better here than I have in a long time. I think it's sleeping in the same room with Toby. I hear his breathing, and it's so peaceful that I fall right to sleep. I haven't done that in a long time."

"You must miss Dad a lot."

"Especially at night. I don't like being alone. If I hear a little noise, I get frightened. I'm nervous all the time."

Lucy nodded. "I know what you mean."

"I wonder if you do. I don't think anybody knows what it's like until it happens to them. Losing a father isn't like losing a husband."

"Maybe," said Lucy, not quite willing to admit that losing her father was insignificant compared with her mother's loss. "What would you like for breakfast?"

"Just an English muffin."

"How about an egg or two? Or some hot cereal?" asked Lucy, eyeing her mother's flat cheeks and stick wrists.

"No, just a muffin. That's what I always have."

"Marmalade?" Lucy asked hopefully.

"That would be nice." The older woman took a sip of coffee. "Lucy, last night I was thinking that I really ought to send some Christmas cards. I wasn't going to, but now I've changed my mind."

Lucy almost dropped the knife she was poking into the marmalade jar. "I think you should. I'm sure you can find some conservative ones."

"I thought I'd look in that gift shop in town and see what they have."

Lucy's heart sank. She wanted to encourage her mother to keep in touch with her friends, but with Sara still sick and a long list of things to do, she felt frantic at the prospect of another trip to town.

"Mom, I'd love to help, but I just can't drive you today."

"I could drive myself. I have a license."

This was news to Lucy. "You do? Dad always drove."

"He did, but I never let my license expire. I've been out a few times and I've done quite well."

"In the city?" Lucy was incredulous.

"Only around the neighborhood, but I'm sure I could manage these roads. There isn't much traffic."

"Okay," Lucy agreed. She certainly wasn't going to discourage her. In fact, new possibilities were opening before her. "Would you mind picking up a few things for me?"

Lucy watched as her mother drove the Subaru very cautiously down the long driveway. As she turned out onto the road a large egg truck swerved to avoid her, narrowly missing a collision, but she continued on her way. Lucy wasn't sure if her mother had noticed or not. She sighed. There was nothing she could do now except send up a quick prayer and keep her fingers crossed. She poured herself a second cup of coffee and sat down with the morning paper. She wanted to find a kitten for the kids to replace poor Patches, so she turned to the classifieds.

The first ad she saw read "Kute, Kuddly, Kristmas Kittens." Lucy chuckled and dialed the number, but the woman who answered told her that the kittens were all gone. She hung up and turned back to the paper to check the next ad. "Free to a good home," it read. "Pretty Calico Kittens."

"I'm calling about the kittens," began Lucy when the woman answered.

"We do have some kittens," the voice admitted cautiously. "But we want to make sure they'll be well taken care of."

"We've had lots of cats. We're very experienced cat owners, and I can promise we'll take good care of the kitten," Lucy promised.

"How many cats do you have?" inquired the voice.

"None at the moment," Lucy confessed. "Our last cat was killed. . . ." The moment she said it she realized her mistake. She should have said "died of old age," but she continued, hoping to convince the kitten owner that she was not a kitten abuser. "Our children have been very upset. They miss old Patches very much, and I was hoping to give them a new kitten for Christmas."

"You have children?" The voice was shocked.

"I'm sorry, but our kittens are not used to children. Good-bye."

Lucy tapped her fingers on the table and looked at the next ad. She scratched her head thoughtfully and thought about Culpepper's ad in *Modern Mercenary* magazine. Someone had read those ads looking for a hit man to kill Sam Miller just as she had gone through the ads looking for a kitten. When she didn't get a satisfactory response, she just went on to the next ad. And whoever had called Culpepper had probably just gone on to the next ad when he'd refused the job.

Lucy dialed the next number. She heard the phone ring six times and was about to hang up when she heard the receiver being picked up. She could hear a baby crying in the background.

"Hello?"

"Hi," piped a child's voice.

"Can I speak to your mommy?"

"Okay." There was a long silence. Lucy thought of the times she'd found the receiver lying on the counter, the caller forgotten, as some distraction interrupted Sara or Elizabeth as they searched for her.

"Hello?" said a grown-up voice.

"I'm calling about the kittens," Lucy said.

"How many do you want?"

"Just one."

"How about two? Two are definitely more fun than one."

"Two would cause fights," said Lucy, suddenly overcome with Christmas spirit. "Do you have three?"

"Sure, come on over."

"I must be crazy," Lucy said, stricken with second thoughts.

"It's Christmas. Live a little! Crystal, put that kitten down!"

Lucy wrote down the directions and told the woman she would come the next day, Christmas Eve. What am I getting myself into? she thought as she replaced the receiver. Three cats. It wasn't all that ridiculous, she tried to convince herself. The house was big, and the kids would be thrilled to have one cat each. Maybe three cats would be content to stay safely at home. Anything was possible. She shuddered involuntarily, thinking of poor Patches and Sam Miller, too.

"I know I shouldn't do this," she said aloud, dialing the police station. When she got Culpepper on the line, she just plunged in.

"Barney, I think I know how we can find Sam Miller's killer."

She explained how the idea had come to her while she had been looking for a kitten in the classifieds. Culpepper was skeptical.

"Lucy, this is crazy. Just let the state police handle it."

"What do you mean? Yesterday you were worried about your job. I'm just trying to help."

"I shouldn't have been crying on your shoulder. This is my problem," insisted Culpepper.

"Do you still have the magazine? I'd love to see the ad."

"You would?" Culpepper was flattered.

"You didn't throw it away, did you?"

"Oh, no, I've still got it," he admitted.

"Well, let's see who else advertised. Maybe one of them was the killer. I can't wait to get started. When can we get together?" she demanded.

"Now, hold on, Lucy. I still think I should handle this by myself."

"Barney, people just hear your voice and they know you're a cop. You need me for this. Besides, I want to make up for suspecting you."

"Lucy—"

"No, Barney, don't 'Lucy' me. Just get over here as soon as you can. I've got all the Pinewood Derby cars. You can pick Eddie's up, and you can show me the ad. Okay? I can't leave the house because Sara's got the flu and my mother took the car."

"And you think you're gonna help me? Some hot-shot detective you are," accused Culpepper.

"Yeah. The original gumshoe, that's me. And when I say gum, I mean Double Bubble." Lucy laughed and bent over to peel a large pink wad from the bottom of her Reebok high-tops.

13

#9137 Fishing the old-fashioned way can be frustrating. This newfangled sonar scanner actually finds and tracks schools of fish so you can put your hook where the fish are. Can be operated with 10 "D" batteries or connected directly to a power source. Solid-state, UL approved. $345.

If Barney Culpepper were a dog, thought Lucy as she opened the kitchen door for him, he would be a Saint Bernard. Doorways were always too small for him and ceilings too low; he had to bend his head as he came through the doorway into the kitchen. As he stood there unzipping his jacket, his cheeks seemed to droop into jowls. Slowly he took off his regulation blue jacket and tossed it on the corner chair, ran his hands through his shaggy brown hair, and squared his burly shoulders before sitting down at the kitchen table.

When Lucy had first met Barney, back in the granola years, she'd thought of him as a typical redneck. He was a recent Vietnam vet, and she'd been a bit leery of him, expecting him to explode into violence whenever he encountered members of the college-educated peace brigade who were moving into Tinker's Cove. But when the battery in the Malibu she'd been driving died one day, he'd gone out of his way to get her car going again. She'd been struck by his quiet, assured helpfulness.

Then she began meeting him on some of the same volunteer committees she was serving on, especially the Cub Scouts and the School Improvement Council. She had come to respect his willingness to work, and his practical approach. He was the sort of man you could count on; sometimes she wished she'd had a big brother like Barney.

She eyed the well-thumbed copy of *Modern Mercenary* that he placed on the table in front of him and gave him the little box containing the Pinewood Derby car kit.

"Eddie won last year, didn't he?" she asked. "He made a fast little car."

"It broke, though, on the last heat. This year he wants to put on a rubber bumper. That kid's always thinking," Barney said proudly.

"You know, I've never seen one of these magazines before," she said, sliding a cup of coffee in front of him and picking up the magazine.

"Now, Lucy. I'm not sure you should get involved in this."

"What do you mean, 'get involved'? I found Sam

Miller's body. I worked for him. I live in this town. I *am* involved, and I'm not just going to shut my eyes and pretend I'm not. I can't let people get killed practically in my backyard. I have a family to raise."

"That's what I mean. Your kids need you. This could be dangerous."

"Don't you think it's dangerous living in a place where people get murdered in their own cars? I won't stand for it," said Lucy, shaking her head. "Besides, Christmas is two days off and I'm going to be cooped up with my mother and Bill's folks, and I'll go crazy if I don't have something else to think about. Where are the ads?"

"In the back," Barney said, capitulating.

Lucy leafed through the magazine quickly, noting the ads for weapons and camouflage suits and the action-packed adventure stories complete with lurid illustrations. There was even a comic strip, *Mercenary Max.* The classified ads were just after the comic.

"You know, this kind of reminds me of *Boy's Life*," Lucy commented absently.

"Naw. *Boy's Life* is for kids. This is for men."

"Oh." Lucy smiled to herself. "Here we are, 'Courageous Captain at your service.' He sounds more like a stud for hire than a hit man."

"He probably is. I got a few calls for that kind of service myself," admitted Barney, blushing.

"You did?" Lucy's voice rose.

"I turned 'em down, of course."

"Hmmm," Lucy said thoughtfully. So much for

Sue's theories. "None of these ads have phone numbers. They're all boxes."

"That's right. If you're a professional killer, you're hardly going to put your phone number in an ad. If you kill somebody, you don't want to leave a trail of phone calls, especially long distance. No, you get a post office box using a false name, or you can have the magazine give you a box number. Then they hold the mail and send it on to you. That's what I had them do."

"So we just have to write to these ads?"

"Yeah, just drop 'em a line, tell 'em to call at a certain time."

"I thought phone calls were out," said Lucy.

"They'll use a pay phone."

"Oh." Lucy rummaged in the Hoosier for paper and envelopes. "Somehow I thought this would be more exciting."

"Let's just hope it doesn't get too exciting. Lucy, you'd better have a good story ready when they call."

"How's this? I want somebody to kill my husband because he's mean to me."

"Mean to you?"

"Say he beats me. Brutally. I saw that on *60 Minutes*."

"Okay. It's a little lame, but hell, I guess it's happened before. How much are you going to offer for doing the job?"

"Twenty-five thousand?"

"Sounds good."

"Do you think they'll go for it?"

"Well, if they do, we've got a possible suspect.

But I don't think most of these ads are genuine. Real hit men probably don't advertise. Most of 'em are probably just guys looking for a little excitement like I was. Or selling sex like Courageous Captain there. But it's worth trying, I guess. After all, somebody did call me." He scratched his chin. "You never know, we might get lucky."

"What do we do then?" Lucy asked.

"Then we take it one step at a time. We can try to set up a meeting. Very carefully. Don't do anything without me." Culpepper's voice was earnest. "I want to keep an eye on things."

"Okay," Lucy agreed. "This guy looks serious. 'Man for Hire. Professional and efficient.' Gives me the willies. What should I write?"

"How about, 'If interested in twenty-five thousand dollars, call . . .' and put down your phone number and the time you want him to call," advised Barney.

Lucy thought for a minute. "I don't want him to call when the kids are home, so it has to be during school hours."

"Now you're thinking like a pro," Barney teased.

"Don't laugh. My kids could scare off the meanest, toughest criminal. And I certainly don't want hit men calling during Christmas when Bill's folks are here. What would they think?"

Barney shook his head. "It'll take a couple of weeks if the mail's forwarded."

Lucy checked her calendar. "How about nine-thirty A.M. on Wednesday, January fifth?"

"Sounds good." Culpepper ran his finger down the column of ads. "Put down 'Man for Hire' at nine-thirty, 'Pest Control'—I don't think he's serious—at ten, and 'Bad Guy' at ten-thirty. Is that enough for one day?"

"We can fit one more in at eleven, but then I have to pick up Sara at nursery school."

" 'Ex-marine' sounds promising, put him down for eleven. Then on Thursday you can have 'Combat Veteran' for nine-thirty and 'Cool Professional' for ten. That's it." He put down the magazine.

"You know," said Lucy, licking an envelope, "this is an awful lot like paying bills."

"A lot of life is like that." Barney smiled ruefully. "I wanted to be a cop because I thought it would be real exciting. High-speed car chases, shoot-outs, the works. Like on TV. You know what I spend most of my time doing? Paperwork! Paperwork and traffic duty. I sure didn't expect that." He shook his head and took a big gulp of coffee.

"You drink too much coffee. It's not good for you."

"Gotta take a risk sometimes, Lucy. Have that extra cup of coffee, drive without a seat belt, have one beer too many. You know what I mean?"

"I do. I always hated Nancy's slogan, 'Just say no.' So prim and proper. I'd rather say yes."

"Lucy, I hope you're not going out on a limb for me." Culpepper was looking straight at her, and the direct eye contact was making her uncomfortable. She shifted on her seat and glanced away.

"Now, don't get all mushy on me, Culpepper. I have an ulterior motive."

"Uh-oh." Now it was Barney's turn to shift uncomfortably on his seat.

"Yup. Pack twenty-seven needs a new cubmaster next year."

"They do?" Culpepper gulped.

"They sure do. I figure you're the perfect man for the job."

"Lucy," said Culpepper, rising and reaching for his jacket, "if I'm not in jail, I'll be glad to do it."

Lucy watched as he drove away, then went upstairs to see how Sara was doing. Her fever was down and she was demanding food, so Lucy set her up on the couch, where she could watch TV and nibble on some toast. Then she put a casserole together for supper and prepared for the afternoon onslaught when Toby and Elizabeth came home from school.

Much to her relief, her mother and the Subaru returned intact. Lucy showed her where the salad fixings were in the refrigerator; then she left for work.

At Country Cousins, she punched the time clock and hung her coat up slowly; ever since the layoffs she hadn't enjoyed going to work. She missed Bev and Karen and the others; the phone room seemed empty without them.

"You know, I used to like working here," Ruthie said as they went to their computers. "The pay wasn't very good, but there used to be a nice atmosphere."

"I know what you mean. Now, I'm always expecting to get laid off, and I don't think I'd mind if I was," admitted Lucy.

"Oh, they won't lay you off. You're a good producer. They always go for the ones who are going to retire or have a baby—the ones who actually use the benefits." Ruthie sounded bitter but resigned.

"Is that why Karen and Bev were laid off? That's terrible."

"Look for yourself, Lucy. You can see who survived the cuts. I haven't noticed any drop in sales, have you? I think they just wanted to get rid of the deadwood."

"Sales always drop off after Christmas," Lucy reminded her.

"But they never had layoffs before. Not when Sam was in charge," Ruthie argued. "Lower payroll means higher profits. This'll be a feather in somebody's cap."

"Do you think George was behind this?"

"Doesn't really matter whose idea it was, does it? The whole board of directors had to approve it. They don't care about people like us." Ruthie clicked on her computer and started pounding away angrily at the keyboard.

Lucy was kept busy all night trying to keep up with the calls. She frequently had several callers waiting, something that had never happened to her before. The customers weren't very pleased at having to wait to place their orders, and by the time she could take her break, her tact was exhausted.

She sat alone in the break room, sipping her diet soda and reading last week's *Pennysaver*. George Higham stopped in the doorway and looked at her, but she shot him such an evil glance that he beat a hasty retreat.

She was sure George had masterminded the layoffs. Ever since Sam Miller's death, George had been the one to watch. His star was certainly ascending, and Lucy thought she knew why. Of all the people at Country Cousins, he seemed to have gained the most from Sam's death. She took a long pull on the can of soda and took a deep breath. She'd love to be able to prove that George had killed Sam.

14

#9001 *Fire starters. These pieces of genuine Georgia fatwood make starting a fire easy and quick. Five pounds in a decorative gift box. $25.*

"It's Christmas Eve! Tomorrow is Christmas!" shouted Toby as he ran into the kitchen.

Lucy finished pouring herself a cup of coffee and smiled at Bill, who was sitting at the table reading the *Herald*.

"You know what they say about Christmas Eve, don't you? It's supposed to be the longest day of the year," Bill said in a teasing voice.

"No, it isn't," answered Toby. "December twenty-first, the day of the winter solstice, is the shortest day. Now the days are short and the nights are long."

"Oh," said Bill. "I must have had it wrong. To me, Christmas Eve always seems longer."

Lucy sighed. "I wish it was the longest day. I need a long day to fit in everything I have to do."

"I want to work on the Dempsey house this morning and make up some of the time I lost earlier this week. I'll try to knock off a little early so I'll be here when my folks arrive."

"Okay. I have to go grocery shopping and do some last-minute errands."

"What about us? What'll we do?" Toby demanded.

"You're going to stay home with Grandma," asserted Lucy. "Maybe she'll show you how to make popcorn chains."

"I have a better idea," said Helen, entering the kitchen and heading straight for the coffeepot. "We'll eat the popcorn and make paper chains."

"Okay," agreed Toby. "That sounds like fun."

Lucy felt light-hearted as she slammed the hatchback shut on twelve brown bags of groceries. She'd put in a busy morning doing a lightning job of housecleaning by dusting the tabletops, fluffing the couch pillows, and bundling all extraneous objects into a large trash bag, which she'd stuffed in the back of her closet. When she'd left the house her mother had been vacuuming the rugs and the girls had been chattering away with her, asking what Christmas was like when she was a little girl. Now Lucy had just one errand left, and that was to pick up the kittens.

She carefully followed the directions she'd been given and soon found herself on a road she didn't

know in a part of town she'd never seen before.
Scattered along the road, like toys left on the living room floor and then forgotten by a careless
child, were worn-out house trailers, shacks constructed from bits and pieces of other buildings,
and an assortment of battered, rusting cars and
trucks. Lucy pulled up in front of a little brown
house with rough-sawn siding that had probably
once been a hunting camp.

She stepped cautiously onto a rotting step and
knocked timidly on the door. She was surprised
when it was opened by a pretty girl with dark hair.
She didn't look more than seventeen, wearing a
bright T-shirt and jeans and balancing a plump,
nearly naked baby on her hip. Her eyes were suspicious and defensive as she looked Lucy over, but
she had an air of vulnerability that Lucy found attractive.

"I've come about the kittens," explained Lucy,
indicating the plastic cat carrier she was holding.

"Oh, great, come on in!" said the girl, revealing
a beautiful, wide smile. She opened the door and
stood aside. "I'm Lisa Young," she said, introduc-
ing herself. "Never mind the house. Honestly,
with this heater it's full blast or nothing. Now,
where are those kittens?"

From her spot by the door Lucy received the full
blast of the heater, but she knew that in really
cold weather the camp, perched as it was on ce-
ment block pilings, must be freezing. She unzipped her jacket and tried not to look as if she
were inspecting the one-room house. Houses like

this were common on the back roads, but she'd never been inside one before.

At first it was difficult to see much. It was dark in the house even though a bare bulb was burning in the center of the ceiling. Sheets of plastic had been taped over the windows to keep out the wind. As her eyes adjusted Lucy saw that the stud cavities had been filled with batts of fiberglass insulation; in places pieces of recycled paneling with worn and rounded edges had been nailed over the insulation. One end of the room was the kitchen, with an early-model propane stove that was also a heater. There was a table covered with an ugly plastic cloth and an assortment of chairs. A tiny plastic tree with twinkling lights stood on the table. There was no sign of running water or even an indoor bathroom. A dented and rusty refrigerator hummed noisily, bearing a picture of a Biafran child. His head was enormous, his eyes huge, and his tiny sticklike arms were crossed over his protruding ribs. Beneath the picture was written, "Before you yell about mac and cheese again, be grateful for what you got."

Lucy swallowed hard and looked at the other end of the room. There an old sheet hung from a length of cord, separating a neatly made double bed from a set of camp-style bunks. All of the beds were covered with handmade log cabin quilts, faded with washing and drying in the sun. Sitting on the top bunk was a tiny little girl, a replica of her mother, with her dark hair and full lips.

"I was playing with the kittens, Ma," she complained.

"It's time to say good-bye to them," Lisa said firmly.

"We'll still have Tiger Lily, right?"

"That's right." She scooped up the kittens and held them against her chest for Lucy to see. "This one here is Midnight because he's black, and this one is Jumbles, and here is Boots. We weren't very original, but we wanted them to have names. You'll probably want to name 'em yourself."

"I'm sure my kids will have some ideas," said Lucy, smiling a bit too broadly. "Let's put them in the carrier, okay? I feel so lucky to have found them. Our cat was killed, and my kids are pretty upset. Having their own kittens will make Christmas special," she gushed, suddenly wondering how this family was going to celebrate Christmas. "Is ten dollars apiece okay with you?"

"What?" Lisa's face was blank.

"Ten dollars. I'm afraid I can't go much higher."

"They're free. I'm just glad to get rid of them. Pet food's expensive and you can't use food stamps for it."

"Well, I won't take them unless you let me pay," said Lucy, holding out three ten-dollar bills.

"Okay. I won't say I can't use the money. Thanks."

As Lucy carried the kittens out to the car, she was overwhelmed with guilt. She'd never thought of herself and Bill as wealthy; every month they had to juggle the bills, and the Visa balance stubbornly refused to shrink. But today the sum of their material possessions embarrassed her.

As she put the kittens on the backseat she noticed a box of candy canes poking out from one of the grocery bags. Remembering the very tiny Christmas tree on the table, she dug a little deeper and pulled out a roasting chicken, aware that she had a freezer full of food at home as well as money in the bank. She rummaged through the other bags and added cranberry sauce, stuffing, potatoes, a few cans of vegetables, and a bottle of apple juice. Looking for something sweet, she shrugged and tossed in a bucket of dastardly mash ice cream. Give till it hurts, she thought.

She was tempted just to leave the bag on the porch, but instead she made herself knock. When the door opened she said, "I'm really so grateful for the kittens, won't you please take these groceries?"

Lisa pulled herself up to her full height and said unsmilingly, "Thank you, but I already have Christmas dinner planned. We're having macaroni."

Lucy smiled encouragingly. "My husband and I had tofu and brown rice for Christmas once. We decided never again. Please take it."

Lisa shrugged and then smiled, accepting the bag of groceries. "Merry Christmas!" she said, and shut the door.

"Now, little kittens, how am I going to keep you a secret until tomorrow?" Pulling the car off the road a few feet before her driveway, Lucy put the carrier on the floor behind the driver's seat and tossed a blanket over it. Then she pulled in the driveway and started unloading the groceries. She carried one bag and a gallon jug of milk into the kitchen, pausing at the door to see if any of the kids were around. She heard a low murmur from the front of the house, so she put the groceries on the table and dashed back to the car. Covering the kittens with the blanket, she ran as quickly as she could back to the kitchen and scooted down the cellar stairs. She put the carrier next to the furnace and, apologizing to the kittens for confining them, was back in the kitchen before the kids realized she was home.

"Help me with the groceries, Toby. Grandma and Grandpa Stone will be here any minute.

"How'd everything go?" she asked her mother.

"Come and see the tree!" demanded Sara. "We made it so pretty."

Helen shrugged. "All right, I guess."

"Well, it sounds as if you've been busy. Let me see the tree," said Lucy, allowing the girls to pull her along.

Just then they heard the crunch of tires on the gravel driveway. Bill's folks had arrived. The house was soon full of confusion and bustle as hugs and kisses were exchanged, groceries put away, and suitcases and shopping bags full of presents carried in.

At last, Bill's parents were settled, and everyone was gathered around a cheerful fire in the living room. The scene looked Christmas card perfect: the lush tree twinkling in the corner, three children playing quietly on the rug, the adults relaxing on the couch and easy chairs. Lucy perched on the edge of her grandfather's cane chair, took a deep breath, and tried to still the butterflies that were churning in her stomach. Now she ought to be able to relax. After working toward it for weeks, Christmas was finally here. The house was clean, the cookies baked, the presents wrapped. Everything was under control, she realized, except for the people. She was so worried that her mother's depression would return and dampen the holiday, or that Bill's father, always unpredictable, would say exactly the wrong thing.

She had always found the elder Mr. Stone intimidating. She would never forget the first time she had met him. She had been terribly nervous and as Bill's fiancée had wanted to make a good impression. She hadn't known what to say when Mr. Stone suggested that she escort Brother, Mrs. Stone's retarded brother, to the bathroom. She could still remember the blood rushing to her face as she stammered out an excuse, and Bill had rushed to her rescue, leading Brother out of the room. That meant she was left alone with Mr. Stone, who'd muttered something and left the room, too. All by herself in the Stones' living room, she had felt totally abandoned and suspected that she had failed some important test.

She had always marveled that Bill's mother never seemed upset by her rude husband. She was a small, plump, cheerful woman who serenely managed to smooth the feathers that her husband continually ruffled. Now she was sitting on the couch with Helen, and the two women were chatting together.

Bill's father was sprawled on the recliner, puzzling over a fishing reel Toby had asked him to fix. Suddenly he looked up and demanded, "Don't you have any cookies? What's Christmas without cookies?"

"I've got cookies." Lucy snapped to attention. "Would you like some coffee or tea to go with them?"

"Sure, whatever," he answered gruffly.

"Tea would be very nice," said Mrs. Stone. "Can I help?"

"No, I can manage. Just relax," answered Lucy.

"Of course, there's only one really good Christmas cookie. You don't have 'em. They're Italian. Called pizza or something."

"Do you mean pizelle?" asked Lucy.

"Yeah. They're made on a little waffle iron thing. Had 'em once and never forgot 'em."

Lucy couldn't help smiling as she went off to the kitchen, because high up on a shelf in the pantry, in her tin of cookies from the cookie exchange, were six lovely pizelle made by Lydia Volpe. Lucy hummed as she put the water on to boil and set out cups. She added three glasses of milk for the children, and then she climbed up the stepladder and carefully brought down the cookies. She arranged them attractively on her special Christmas plate, clustering the delicate pizelle together. When the kettle shrieked she poured the tea and proudly carried the tray out of the kitchen. She couldn't wait to see the expression on Grandpa Stone's face.

15

#4840 New Englanders have long known the luxury of 100% cotton flannel sheets. Warm to the touch, flannel ensures a good night's sleep. Each set includes one fitted sheet, one flat sheet, and two cases. In blue, yellow, or ecru. Specify twin, $29; double, $39; queen, $49; or king, $59.

Christmas Eve really is the longest day of the year, thought Lucy as she glanced at the kitchen clock on her way to bed. It was two in the morning and Bill was still snapping together the dozens of interlocking pieces of the Barbie town house. Everything else was ready. The presents were arranged under the tree, the stockings were filled, and Santa had nibbled his cookies and poured his warm milk down the kitchen drain. The house was quiet; everyone was asleep, presumably dreaming of sugarplums. Lucy went down to the cellar to get the kittens.

She found them all asleep in a pile in a corner of the cardboard box she'd made their temporary home. She picked up the carton and tiptoed upstairs with it. Setting it down next to her bed, she climbed between the sheets and put all three kittens in her lap.

"Time for some exercise," she told them, and smiled as they climbed clumsily over each other and explored the mysterious hills and valleys her legs made in the covers. She picked each one up and examined it carefully, relieved to find they all appeared healthy, with no sign of fleas.

"Well, what have we got here?" asked Bill, coming into the room and beginning to strip off his clothes.

"Christmas kittens," said Lucy, admiring the long, lean curve of his back as he bent over and pulled on his pajama pants. "How are we going to manage this? We can't really put them in the kids' stockings."

"Never you worry," Bill boasted. "No job is too difficult for Super-Santa!"

"You are a super Santa. Did Barbie's house go together okay?"

"Nothing to it." Bill shrugged. "Fifteen pages of directions, innumerable tiny plastic parts, all pink; anyone with a degree in engineering could do it in five hours, easy."

Lucy laughed. "Don't expect to get any credit. You know what Toby told me? He says he doesn't really believe in Santa, but he can't believe we'd spend that much money on presents!"

"Well, I can see his point. All year long we say, 'You can't have that because it's too expensive,' then at Christmas it's all under the tree." He lifted the covers to climb into bed, and the kittens all tumbled into Lucy's lap.

She laughed and handed one to Bill. "Aren't they sweet?"

"Almost as sweet as you," said Bill, nuzzling her neck. "Boy, Dad sure loved those cookies."

"I think it's the first time I've managed to do anything that pleased him. I was worried he'd choke on those pizelle."

"When he absolutely has to, he can say something nice. He's a lot happier, though, when he can find something to criticize." Bill shook his head. "It's too bad. When I was a kid I used to knock myself out trying to please him. I was never good enough for him. If I got a base hit, it should have been a home run. If I got a ninety-five, it should have been a hundred. That's probably why I became a hippie carpenter instead of an insurance underwriter like him."

"You'd be a terrible insurance underwriter," said Lucy, stroking his hand. "You're a good father."

"I don't want to be like him. I make mistakes, but they're not the same ones he made. If Toby strikes out, I tell him he looked good up there. I tell him even Pete Rose strikes out. I tell him he'll get a piece of it next time."

Lucy snuggled up to him. "How about a piece of it right now?"

"Nope. I'm a liberated modern man. I'm not afraid to admit that I'm too tired."

"Poor Santa. Well, kittens, it's time to go to sleep." She put them back in their box one by one and tucked the box in a corner of the room. Then she hopped back into the warm bed and curled around Bill. Nestled together, they were both asleep before they knew it.

16

#6175 These practical cushions for pets are filled with cedar shavings to repel fleas. The removable cover is machine washable and comes in green, red, or plaid. Three sizes: small, $25; medium, $39; and large, $60.

"Mommy, can I go downstairs and see if Santa came?" Toby's whisper was so earnest that Lucy had to smile as she groped for the clock.

"It's six o'clock," he assured her. The family rule was that nobody woke up Mommy and Daddy before six.

"Okay, but be quiet. Don't wake your grandparents. Elizabeth, you go, too, and help carry the stockings."

Lucy sat up and rubbed her eyes. She yawned and smiled at Bill. "I feel as though I just got to sleep."

"I'll make coffee," Bill volunteered, climbing out of bed.

"Sara, hop in here. You must be freezing without your slippers."

Soon the whole family was gathered in the sleigh bed. Lucy and Bill sipped coffee and smiled indulgently while the children pulled small treasures from their stockings. Reaching into a stocking and finding an oddly shaped, mysterious package—to Lucy that was what Christmas was all about.

"What's this?" asked Sara, holding up a little catnip mouse.

"It's a cat toy," Toby informed her. "Santa must have made a mistake."

"Maybe Santa hasn't heard about Patches," Elizabeth said reasonably.

"Or maybe he knows something you don't," said Bill thoughtfully.

"What's that box doing in the corner?" said Lucy. "I didn't put it there."

"I'll see," Toby shouted, jumping out of bed. "It's kittens! Three of them!"

"Careful, Toby," Lucy cautioned as he picked up the carton and brought it over to her. "Look, Santa brought one for each of you. Now, who wants the little orange one?"

"Oh, I do." Sara sighed and reached for the soft furry bundle.

"Be gentle. Remember, he's just a baby," said Bill.

"Mom, I want the black one. The black one should go to a boy," Toby argued.

"Okay. That leaves the calico one for you, Elizabeth. Is that okay?"

"Oh, yes." Elizabeth sighed. "Calico cats are always girls."

"Well, that worked out well," Lucy said. "What are you going to name them?"

"I'm naming mine 'Softy,' " said Sara, " 'cause he's so soft."

"I'm naming mine 'Mac' 'cause he's so tough," said Toby, holding up a very tiny fluff of black fur with two bright eyes.

"I'm going to wait until I know my kitten better before I name her," said Elizabeth. "This is the best Christmas ever."

"I'm sure Santa wants you to take good care of your kittens," Bill announced. "No rough stuff, make sure they get plenty to eat and lots of rest. Okay, gang?"

As she leaned back against the pillows, watching the children dangle Christmas ribbons for the kittens to chase, Lucy rubbed her eyes and yawned again. Bill put his arm around her shoulder and gave her a squeeze as Bill's father appeared in the doorway.

"So, you started Christmas without me? What have you got here, kittens? Well, don't do another thing until you open my present," he said, producing a large, gaily wrapped box.

"You want us to open this now?" said Bill.

"Right away."

"But Mom's not up," Bill protested.

"Doesn't matter. Open it up," he ordered.

Bill shrugged and began to open the package but

stopped in amazement when he realized what it was.

"This is a video camera," he said as if there were some mistake.

"That's right. You can film the whole day. Hurry up! You're missing some cute shots of the kids and the kittens."

"Okay, okay. Just let me figure it out."

"It's ready to go. All you have to do is push that red button."

"Really?"

"Yeah. They're great. Fantastic gadgets." The older man bounced around them, barely able to restrain himself from grabbing the camera.

Lucy protested, "You really shouldn't have done this. They're so expensive."

"Nonsense. You only go around once, right? Can't take it with you," said Bill senior. "Besides, Edna wants videos of the kids so she can show off to her friends."

Lucy laughed, then threw up her hands in horror as Bill turned the camera on her. "Don't, Bill! I haven't even combed my hair yet."

"Doesn't matter. It looks like Christmas. It looks just like Christmas should."

Indeed, the day was just the way Christmas should be. Eventually the two grandmothers appeared in their robes, with their faces washed and hair combed. Forewarned about the video camera, both had dabbed on some lipstick.

Lucy served coffee and juice while the grandparents opened their stockings, and then everyone moved into the family room to open presents.

After waiting such a long time for Christmas, the children hurried through their piles of gifts, ripping off the paper as fast as they could. Toby was fascinated with the giant insects Lucy had found and was also quite taken with the football his grandfather gave him, but he swore he would never wear the argyle sweater Aunt Madeline had sent him. The girls shook their heads over the red sweaters Aunt Madeline had sent them, but they adored the Barbie house, and the dolls, and the ice skates, and all the other wonderful presents they found under the tree.

The grown-ups opened their packages at a more leisurely pace, stopping to admire each new treasure. Lucy was relieved that Bill approved of the red dress she'd bought at The Carriage Trade, especially after she tried it on for him. Bill senior declared he couldn't wait to try out the fly-tying kit, and both grandmothers immediately draped their scarves over their robes. Lucy was extremely touched by a lovely pair of gold earrings from her mother.

"I wanted to give you something special. I don't know what I would have done without you," her mother said, her eyes glistening with tears.

Lucy worried that the day might be too much for Helen, reminding her of all the Christmases she had shared with her husband. She disappeared for quite a while to get dressed, and when she finally reappeared, she seemed withdrawn and quiet.

"Helen, how about a game of Ping-Pong?" invited Edna. "Elizabeth needs a partner."

To Lucy's surprise, Helen joined the game and even seemed to enjoy herself. Toby and his father and grandfather all went outside to try out Toby's new archery set, and Lucy fussed over the roast.

At four o'clock the family gathered around the long harvest table for Christmas dinner. Candles shone in crystal holders, the silver gleamed, and the centerpiece of golden glass balls and holly sparkled. The children were dressed in their best clothes, Bill and his dad wore their new plaid sport shirts, and the women were all wearing touches of red. Lucy served the roast beef and Yorkshire pudding; dinner was perfect, even the gravy. Lucy had made chocolate mousse from a recipe Sue Finch guaranteed was foolproof, and everyone adored it.

Finally, when the dishes were all done and put away, and the children changed into their new pajamas, they sat around the TV and watched a replay of the day on the VCR.

"Honestly, this ought to be titled *The Perfect Christmas*," said Edna.

"I know," Lucy agreed. They looked up as Bill came into the room.

"Lucy, there's a phone call for you."

When Lucy picked up the receiver she was surprised to hear a male voice on the other end.

"Mrs. Stone, this is Officer Findlay. I'm calling for Mrs. Culpepper. Her husband's been hurt and she wants you to stay with Eddie so she can go to the hospital."

"Of course," said Lucy. "Is he badly hurt?"

"I can't say. I'm not even sure he's alive. His car went off the road near Barrow's Light."

"Oh, my God," Lucy said with a gasp. "I'll be there as soon as I can."

17

#5714 *Shaker stitch hat and scarf set is knitted
from 100% virgin wool yarn. This classic style is
comfortable and warm. One size. Red, blue, or
green. $21.*

As Lucy sped through the night in her little car,
she repeated over and over, "Please let Barney be
all right, let Barney be all right." The car was
frigid; the drive was too short for it to warm up,
and Lucy's stomach tightened as her hands
clenched the wheel. When she pulled up in front
of the little ranch house, she was shivering from
cold and anxiety.

She tapped on the door and stood blinking in
the light and heat that hit her when it was thrown
open. Marge looked terrible. Always a large
woman, she had given up the struggle to contain
her weight some years ago. But now in spite of her

bulk she suddenly seemed frail and vulnerable. Her face was pasty white, and the harsh overhead light revealed dark circles under her eyes.

"Don't worry, Marge," said Lucy, rushing to hug her friend. "I'll stay as long as you need."

"Thanks, Lucy." Marge stepped back but grasped her hands. "I hate to take you from your family at Christmas."

Feeling Marge's hands trembling, Lucy gave them a gentle squeeze. "Don't be silly—it can't be helped. I'm glad you called. Honest. Now, get going," she said, giving her a little shove. "And call me as soon as you have any news."

Lucy stood in the doorway for a moment, watching Officer Findlay lead Marge down the icy path to the patrol car; then she shut the door firmly against the dark and cold. She tiptoed down the hall. It wasn't difficult to figure out which room was Eddie's. Pausing outside the door that had been left slightly ajar, she peeked in. Enough light from the hall filtered in so that she could see Eddie sleeping peacefully. His face was plump and round, and asleep he looked much younger than he did in the daytime. Although he was a big, strapping boy, he wasn't really very old—only ten, like Toby. He still needed his parents, thought Lucy. Both his parents.

Returning to the living room, Lucy sat down on the plaid Herculon couch. She drew her knees up to her chest and hugged them. She was still shivering slightly, and she let out a long, quavering sigh.

The Christmas tree stood in the corner, glimmering as the tinsel wafted gently in the updraft from the baseboard heat. The lights were still on, twinkling gaily, and the opened presents were spread out beneath the pine branches. Among the presents she noticed a hat and scarf set from Country Cousins. It was one of the less expensive items in the catalog and was a very popular gift. Lucy alone had sold hundreds of them. Seeing a little gift card tucked in the corner of the box, she took it out and unfolded it carefully. "To Marge," the card read, "because you need more than love to keep you warm." It was signed "Barney."

Lucy dropped it as if it had suddenly burst into flame in her hand and wrapped her arms around herself. Her glance fell on the worn recliner in the corner that was clearly Barney's chair. The lamp table beside it was well stocked with the hard candies he had sucked on steadily since giving up smoking, and his *TV Guide* and remote control awaited his return.

"Damn," muttered Lucy. She didn't for a moment believe that Barney's crash had been an accident. He was an expert driver; in fact, he'd taken many specialized driving courses for police officers. He loved driving the big cruiser with its antilock brakes and heavy-duty suspension, and often said that if you knew what to do, you could control any skid.

Of course, the road to Barrow's Light was full of curves, and black ice was always possible this time of year. But Barney would have known that and driven accordingly, thought Lucy.

She rose awkwardly to her feet and went out to

the kitchen, remembering the many hours she'd spent babysitting as a teenager. Then, as now, the refrigerator had an undeniable appeal. Marge wouldn't mind if she had a snack. Pulling open the door, she peered in; the remains of the Christmas turkey were wrapped carefully in aluminum foil. Lucy took out the packet and placed it on the table. In the breadbox she found a loaf of homemade bread, and the covered butter dish was placed nearby. Lucy smiled approvingly. She hated refrigerated butter herself and always kept her butter out, except in the hottest days of summer.

With nothing else to do except worry about Barney, she made a project of constructing a sandwich, slicing two perfectly even pieces of bread. She put them in the toaster and watched carefully so she could take them out when they were just lightly toasted. Then she spread them with the soft butter, covering even the corners and watching the butter melt into the little airholes. Taking out a large carving knife, she cut two thin slices of breast meat and laid them on the bread. She dusted the meat with salt and pepper, then fished a head of lettuce out of the crisper and peeled off a nicely wrinkled leaf. Adding this to the sandwich, she placed the second piece of bread on top. With geometric precision she cut the sandwich from corner to corner in four triangles. Opening the refrigerator again, she pulled out a bottle of Moosehead Ale, then sat down at the table to eat her snack.

What if the cruiser had some sort of mechanical failure? It was possible, but unlikely. Barney and the other cops maintained the cruisers themselves, in a garage underneath the police station. They didn't trust the black-and-whites to just any mechanic; they knew their lives could depend on the cars and followed a strict maintenance schedule religiously.

Could the car have been sabotaged? Could someone have cut the brake line? Lucy didn't think so. The saboteur would have been taking an enormous risk, unless he was someone the cops knew well—someone who was above suspicion or perhaps someone who was interested in cars. Lucy couldn't get away from the fact that Sam Miller had been killed in a car, and Barney had almost been killed in his.

Lucy chewed her sandwich and sipped her beer thoughtfully. The last time she'd seen Barney he'd been brimming with life, complaining that his job was boring. Had he finally gotten the high-speed chase he'd wanted? She suspected that whether he knew it or not, he'd discovered something that made him dangerous to Sam Miller's murderer. And whatever it was, it had driven the murderer to attempt a second killing.

If he died, how was Marge going to manage? Now, more than ever, families needed two incomes to get by. In her heart Lucy knew that security was just an illusion. She'd never fallen into the trap her mother had of building her life completely around her husband. Down deep she knew there was only one person she could count on—herself. Paychecks, houses, husbands, children, could all be lost in an instant. There are no certainties in life except death, she thought. We are all on slippery ground indeed.

Tragedy, however, was no excuse for leaving dirty dishes. Lucy washed up the dish and knife she'd used and wiped the table. She found a piece of paper and a pencil and began making a list of people who could help Marge. Checking the clock, she realized it was only a little bit past nine, not too late to call Sue.

"Hi, Sue—it's me, Lucy. Did you have a good Christmas?"

"Did I? You'll never guess what Tom gave me—a gorgeous aviator's jacket."

"Lucky you. But I didn't call to compare Christmas presents. Something terrible's happened."

"What's the matter?" Sue's voice was immediately full of concern.

Lucy told her the news, including the few details she knew about Barney's crash.

"I just can't believe it. What a terrible thing, especially at Christmas."

"I know. It's awful here in their house. All the presents are under the tree and everything."

"Marge will need a lot of help. Her mother's been sick and she doesn't have any other relatives around here."

"She'll need someone to take care of Eddie," said Lucy.

"He's good friends with Adam Stillings. Maybe Pam will take him tomorrow."

"That's a good idea. I better get off the phone and leave the line free. Marge promised to call."

"Okay. I'll give Pam a call tonight. Adam's probably covering the accident for the *Pennysaver*."

"Let me know if you hear anything, okay?"

Lucy replaced the receiver and tiptoed down the hall to make sure she hadn't disturbed Eddie. Seeing that he was still sleeping deeply, she went back to the kitchen. She stood leaning against the kitchen sink, savoring the last drops of beer and reading the collection of notices attached to the refrigerator with magnets.

There was a birthday party invitation printed with brightly colored dinosaurs; an identical one was on Lucy's refrigerator. Toby and Eddie and the rest of the Cub Scout den had been invited to Rick Goodman's birthday party. The school calendar and the lunch menus for December were neatly clipped in a magnetic holder, along with the rules for constructing the little Pinewood Derby cars the Cub Scouts would race in January. Lucy made a mental note to have Bill help Eddie since Barney wouldn't be able to. There was a postcard from Opryland that an Aunt Liz had sent last August and a photograph of Barney dressed as a giant bumblebee, which made Lucy grin.

She yawned and glanced at the clock. It was almost ten. She was exhausted, she realized; she had had only a few hours of sleep last night. She checked the TV listings and decided to watch the last hour of *It's a Wonderful Life*. Stretching out on the couch with an afghan over her, she watched only a little bit of the movie before she fell asleep.

Thanks to the Moosehead, she woke up around midnight to go to the bathroom. She switched off the TV and turned off all the lights except for the hall and the outside porch light in case Marge came home. She returned to the couch, and next thing she knew sunlight was streaming through the picture window and the phone was ringing.

"Unnnh," said Lucy in the direction of the receiver.

"Lucy, it's Marge. Did I wake you?"

"That's okay. How's Barney?"

"They took us to Portland last night in the air ambulance. He was in surgery for five hours and I guess they've put him back together. They say he'll recover well from his physical wounds. The problem is that he's in a coma. He could come out of it anytime, or not at all. We just have to wait."

"That's awful!" Lucy blurted.

"I know. I'm just trying to be glad he's alive. I'm not giving up hope. He's strong. They said nine out of ten wouldn't have survived the surgery."

"He'll be fine, Marge, I know he will," said Lucy, struggling to keep her voice from breaking.

"I'll probably be home this afternoon. I'm going to catch some sleep now, and then Dave Davidson is going to bring me home. He's coming up after services this morning. I hate to ask—but could you keep Eddie?"

"It's no problem. Everyone will want to help."

Indeed, Lucy could see through the kitchen window that a car was pulling up in front of the house. A short figure climbed out and began walking toward the house carrying a foil-covered dish.

"In fact, here comes Franny Small. I bet she's got a dish of Austrian ravioli for you."

"I bet she does." Marge laughed weakly. "It's good to know I can depend on people."

"You know you can always depend on Franny to bring Austrian ravioli." Lucy chuckled. "Don't worry about things here. Just take care of yourself and Barney."

Lucy opened the door for Franny. "Goodness, you're up and about early, Franny. Want some coffee?"

"No, thanks, I have to get Mother to church at eight for choir practice. I had this in the freezer and thought Marge might be able to use it. It's Austrian ravioli."

Lucy stifled a smile. "That's so sweet of you, Franny. It's still frozen, so I think I'll just put it in the freezer. Goodness knows when Marge will get back."

"I've got to run, Lucy. Mother hates to be late."

Lucy was making herself a cup of instant coffee when Eddie appeared in the kitchen, barefoot and in pajamas.

"Where's Mom?"

"Your mom and dad were called away on an emergency last night, Eddie. I spent the night here. What do you usually have for breakfast?"

"Scrambled eggs."

"I'll mix 'em up while you get dressed," Lucy said cheerfully. "And be sure to put something on your feet."

While she cooked Lucy wondered how to tell Eddie the bad news. She wanted to get some food in him before she told him, and she wanted him to have something else to think about. She quickly dialed Pam Stillings and asked if Eddie could spend the day with Adam.

Eddie soon reappeared, dressed in new Christmas clothes. Lucy set a plate in front of him and sipped her coffee while she watched him eat.

"Did you have a good Christmas, Eddie? What did Santa bring?"

"Electronic football. I really wanted that."

"Sounds like fun. Maybe you could take it over to Adam's house. I'm going to drop you off there on my way home, okay?"

"Sure. Where are Mom and Dad?"

"Eddie, your dad had an accident last night." Lucy spoke softly. "They took him to the hospital in Portland. Your mom called a little while ago. Your dad had surgery, and he did real well, but he's still unconscious. He's a big strong man, Eddie, and I think he'll be fine."

"Dad once lifted a car off a little girl."

"I remember that," said Lucy. "It was on the TV news."

"Yeah." Eddie's eyes shone with pride.

"Well, he'll probably be in the news again. Meanwhile, you're going to Adam's. Mom will be home later, and you'll probably have leftover turkey for supper. Do you like that?"

"Yeah." Eddie nodded, swallowing hard.

"Let's get a move on," said Lucy. "How about combing your hair and brushing your teeth?"

"Do I have to?"

Lucy raised an eyebrow and smiled to herself as Eddie headed down the hall. The phone was ringing again, and she could see Bev Thompson coming up the walk carrying a pie basket.

18

#8260 *Everything you need to begin cross-country skiing. Fiberglass skis with polyurethane foam cores are extremely durable. Fish-scale provides traction and does not require waxing. Bindings are adjustable to all snow boots. Fiberglass poles are sturdy and lightweight. Blue. $139.*

"I couldn't believe it when I heard," said Bev, shaking her head. "I was going to take this pie to the Friendship Circle dinner tonight, but I've got time to make another one. It's apple."

"Thanks. I know Eddie will enjoy it." Lucy took the pie, and as Bev turned to go she spoke impulsively. "Do you have a minute? I'd love to have a cup of coffee with you."

"Sure, Lucy. I've been missing you and the other girls at work." Bev settled herself at the kitchen table, and Lucy poured two cups of coffee.

"Have you been thinking about getting another job?" Lucy asked.

"Not really. Fred left me well provided for," Bev admitted, taking a sip of coffee. "Actually, I'm thinking of traveling a little. I'd like to visit my son in D.C. Then I could go on to Florida and stay with my sister for a while—she's always after me to come. Then if I flew to San Francisco where my daughter lives and stayed with her a while, winter would be pretty well over." Bev raised an eyebrow and tapped her mug, waiting for Lucy's reaction.

"I'm speechless," said Lucy, smiling. "You've never been one for traveling."

"I know," admitted Bev. "I was perfectly happy to stay here. But now that I don't have my job anymore, there's nothing to keep me here."

Lucy nodded. "Have you seen Karen?"

"I have. She's really mad. Thinks they laid her off because of the baby. Something about the insurance."

"She said she was only working to get the insurance."

"I know," agreed Bev. "She's taking the company to court."

"Really? Good for her." Lucy chuckled. "I don't think the company should get away with it. There were never layoffs when Sam was in charge. I think George was behind it."

"I never liked him. At least now I don't have to be polite to him." She paused. "I saw him, you know. In MacReed's. I didn't say a word to him. I just glared at him." She blushed, remembering her rudeness.

"What were you doing in MacReed's?" asked Lucy. MacReed's was a bait and gun shop.

"Oh, I was seeing about selling Arthur's guns and fishing tackle. I'll certainly never use them, and the money would come in handy for the trip. It was odd seeing George there. I never thought of him as the sporting type."

"What was he doing there?"

"I don't know. He was in the gun side of the shop, though. Maybe he thinks he better get himself some protection now that he's laid off half the town."

"Mrs. Stone, can I watch TV?" Eddie's hair showed signs of recent combing, and there were dribbles of toothpaste on his shirt.

"Sure. Come here a minute." Lucy rubbed at the stains with a damp corner of a kitchen towel. "We'd better get this show on the road."

Bev, quick to take a hint, rose to her feet and began putting on her coat. "Be sure to tell Marge that I'd be happy to help. All she has to do is call."

"I'll do it. Take care, now." Lucy closed the door and started washing up the dishes. It didn't take long for her to tidy up the little house, folding the afghan on the couch, straightening Eddie's bed, and giving the bathroom and kitchen a quick wipe. She wanted it to look nice for Marge when she returned.

Then she had Eddie pack up some toys and they drove over to the Stillingses' house. Pam opened the door for them, smiling her huge smile and welcoming them in a voice that could probably be heard in Alaska.

"Hi, Eddie," she shrieked. "Adam's playing in the living room."

"What did you tell him?" she whispered loudly to Lucy as Eddie made his way down the hall.

Lucy shrugged and smiled apologetically. "I'm operating on a 'need to know' basis. I told him his dad had an accident, he's in the hospital, and that his mother's with him. I told him she'd be home this afternoon. I tried to keep things as normal for him as I could."

"Good." Pam nodded approvingly. She belonged to a generation that took their children's mental health as seriously as their temperatures. "It's best to let Marge decide how much to tell him. Just as long as he doesn't think the accident was his fault."

As she spoke, Pam gave up trying to whisper and her voice rose to its usual piercing decibel. Lucy had often thought Pam's loud voice, and her understanding of child psychology, were the remnants of her brief career as a nursery school teacher.

"The most important thing," she said, concluding her lecture, "is to maintain his usual routine. Children find that very reassuring." She moved aside so her husband could get through the door.

"Hi, Lucy. Good-bye, Lucy," said Ted. The two women watched him stride down the path toward his car, his reporter's notebook sticking out of his back pocket and his camera bag slung over his shoulder.

"Ted's been so excited, having a big story," confided Pam. "There's never even been a murder in

Tinker's Cove before this. Ted says the police are very suspicious about Barney's accident."

"You mean someone tried to kill him?"

"That's what they think. After all, Barney had driven that route at least once a day for fifteen years or more. There's no way he could have made a wrong turn. And the car had just had a complete overhaul, so they're certain it wasn't a mechanical failure. They think it must have been attempted murder. First Sam Miller and now Barney!"

"I was thinking the same thing," admitted Lucy.

"Well, you can read all about it in the *Pennysaver*."

"I will," Lucy promised, giving Pam a wave.

As she drove home Lucy wondered about what Pam had said. Ted generally had a pretty good idea of what was going on in Tinker's Cove. After all, he was the editor, publisher, and chief reporter for the weekly paper that featured ads, coupons, and local news. In Tinker's Cove news generally came from two sources: the town hall and the police and fire departments. Ted covered it all, sitting through interminable evening meetings of the school board, the finance committee, the zoning board of appeals, and the selectmen. Nobody knew more about town politics than he did. Whenever the police and fire departments were called, Ted was there, writing up the automobile accidents, chimney fires, and petty crimes that had been all that filled the log books until now.

The last violent crime in Tinker's Cove had happened in 1881 when a hired man killed Mrs. Flora Kenney with an ax he happened to be holding in a dispute over wages. He had been chopping wood at the time. Immediately overcome with remorse, he'd obligingly hanged himself in the apple orchard. At least, that's how the story went. Anyway, it had happened a very long time ago.

Ted had written a feature story about the Tinker's Cove ax murder, and Lucy had enjoyed reading it. It had seemed more like fiction than fact, until she'd stumbled on the grave of Flora Kenney, "Beloved Wife and Mother," in the cemetery one day last summer. Flora had been real, just like Sam and Barney. The difference was that Flora had been killed in a fit of temper. Whoever killed Sam and Barney had been cold and calculating.

On the other hand, thought Lucy, pulling into the driveway, you couldn't be sure. Perhaps Barney *had* hit a patch of black ice. The road to Barrow's Light was notorious.

As she braked, she saw Bill's father carrying a load of suitcases and bags to his car.

"You're not leaving already?" Lucy protested.

"I'm afraid so. I've got work tomorrow, you know."

"Tomorrow's Monday. I'd forgotten. I was hoping we'd have a longer visit."

Bill grunted as he lifted a heavy suitcase. "We'll be back soon. Edna's got some crazy idea about cross-country skiing. Probably break her leg."

Bill senior stood back to admire his packing job.

Even though his large sedan had a huge trunk, he prided himself on getting the bags stowed perfectly.

"It's just like walking," Lucy reassured him.

"At our age, even walking is risky," he complained. "One slip and you're out of commission with a broken hip."

"Excuses, excuses," Edna chided, advancing with a shopping bag of Christmas loot. "You're just lazy." She turned to Bill, taking the bag he was carrying for her. "He just wants to stay home and play with the VCR."

"We'll send you lots of videos, I promise, but we'd love to have you stay longer."

"I'm hoping I can pry him loose Presidents' Day weekend. I'll threaten him with the coat sales." Edna laughed and gave Lucy and Bill each a peck on the cheek.

They stood arm in arm, watching the salt-stained car disappear down the driveway. Feeling suddenly weary, Lucy leaned against Bill for a moment, luxuriating in the knowledge that he was there to support her.

"Tough night?" he murmured, wrapping his arms around her.

"Not too bad. What's up here?"

"Not much. The usual day-after-Christmas mess."

Entering the house through the back door, Lucy was relieved to see that her mother had the kitchen firmly in hand. She had just started the dishwasher and was wiping the counters.

"Did you have breakfast? There's some stollen," she told Lucy.

"I cooked a huge breakfast for Eddie, but I forgot to eat any myself. I'd love some stollen, and a big glass of milk. Don't bother, I'll get it."

"No, go on in and sit down. I'll fix it for you."

Lucy stepped carefully over the Christmas presents that were scattered across the floor and collapsed on the couch, propping her feet on the coffee table. Toby was too engrossed in his video game to do more than say, "Hi, Mom," but the girls shrieked and jumped up as soon as they saw her. They perched on either side of her and showed her their favorite new Barbie outfits. Lucy sipped her milk and chewed her cake, watching Bill as he cleaned out the fireplace. For once she didn't feel compelled to clean up the Christmas mess; she'd do that later. For now she was positively enjoying the disorderly house, her children, her mother, and, most of all, her husband.

Christmas week passed in a blur. The children were busy with visits to friends and excursions to the movies and the ice-skating rink. Lucy kept in touch with Marge, but the news was always the same. Barney's physical condition continued to improve, but he remained deeply comatose. Marge brought in newspaper articles that she thought would interest him and read them aloud; she even read *Peanuts* to him. She took in photographs of Eddie, and she played his favorite Jimmy Buffett and George Thorogood songs on a portable tape player, but he remained stolidly unreachable.

On New Year's Eve Lucy drove her mother to the airport. They went alone, partly because Lucy didn't want another long wait with the children in tow, but also because she wanted a chance to talk with her mother.

"How are you doing?" Lucy asked as they drove along the highway. "I don't want your polite answer, I want to know how you're *really* doing."

"Well, I don't like the way things are, but I'm all right."

"I was very worried about you when you came. You seemed so depressed."

"I almost didn't come," admitted the older woman. "I was afraid it would be too painful. But there's so much going on at your house that I forgot to worry."

"What do you worry about?"

"Everything! The car, the house, the furnace, the roof. I've never had to think about those things before. What if something breaks?"

"Just call the plumber or the mechanic," Lucy sensibly advised.

"But the expense," her mother protested.

"You've got plenty of money. I think you're really worried about yourself—whether you can cope without Daddy."

"I miss him so much. I still expect him to walk through the door at five-thirty every night."

"I keep seeing men who remind me of him," confided Lucy. "I'll be in a parking lot and I'll see a man who holds his head a certain way, or who has a cap like Daddy used to wear, or a red-and-black plaid jacket. For a second I'll think it's him. Then I remember, and I feel so sad. It must be much worse for you." Lucy glanced at the shriveled figure beside her.

"It's awful. But I know I've got to pick up and get going. Maybe I'll volunteer at the Red Cross or something."

"That's a good idea," Lucy encouraged.

Helen managed a shrug and a wan smile. When it came time to board the plane, Lucy gave her an awkward hug and stood watching as her mother made her careful way through the gate, never turning to look back.

Later that night, Lucy and Bill went out to a movie, and on the way home they stopped at a package store and bought a bottle of champagne. The inexperienced babysitter hadn't been able to get the kids to bed, so they all sat together on the couch and watched TV, counting down as the ball dropped at Times Square. Lucy gave the kids tiny liqueur glasses of champagne, and they felt very grown-up as they drank a toast to the new year.

On New Year's Day Lucy, Bill, and the kids watched the Tournament of Roses parade and took down the Christmas tree. With the tree gone and the presents put away, the house suddenly seemed much bigger. Lucy was looking forward to Monday, when life would return to normal. Bill would go off to work, Toby and Elizabeth would ride the yellow bus to school, and she would drop Sara off at nursery school. Then she would take down the Christmas cards and decorations, she would clean out cupboards and drawers, she would prepare the house for the long winter ahead.

19

#8071 Deluxe sport watch is highly accurate and reliable for field and travel. Quartz crystal ensures it never needs winding. Date indicator and full sweep second hand, luminous dial for night readings. Nylon wrist strap, tan only. Specify man's or woman's model. $39.95.

The cleaning frenzy began as soon as Lucy had the house to herself. She scrubbed the bathroom, mopped the kitchen floor, and changed all the beds. She sorted through the kids' clothes and toys, bagging up the outgrown and tossing out the worn, torn, and broken. She took all the cushions out of the chairs and sofas and found crumpled foil candy wrappers, a small plastic Toto figure, and eighty-seven cents in change. She didn't know what to do with the Christmas cards, so she bundled them together and tucked them away in the bottom desk drawer. The washing machine and dryer hummed steadily in the background as she cleaned and tidied the old farmhouse. She tossed out last year's magazines, unearthed the lemon oil and rubbed the antiques until they gleamed, and replaced the battered old poinsettias with fresh house plants.

On Wednesday morning she was on her knees in the kitchen, emptying the cupboards so she could replace the lining paper. When the phone rang she rose awkwardly to her feet and stepped carefully around the pots, pans, and small appliances that were spread out on the floor.

Expecting the caller to be one of her neighbors, she was surprised when a deep male voice said, "This is Man for Hire."

"What?" said Lucy, noticing that there was quite a thick layer of dust on top of the wall phone.

"You answered my ad," the voice growled. "Man for Hire."

"Oh," said Lucy, realization dawning. "Man for Hire. How nice of you to call. And so punctually, too," she added, noting that the Regulator read precisely nine-thirty. "That's important, I think. Punctuality is desirable in this matter."

I sound like a fool, thought Lucy. This is harder than I thought. I've got to get to the point.

"I'll get right to the point," she said, unconsciously repeating herself. "The reason I need your services is that I'm not happy with my husband."

"That's not an unusual problem, ma'am," rumbled the voice. "If you employ me, you will find that I make every effort to satisfy. I never let my ladies down.''

"You work only for women? Isn't that odd?" asked Lucy.

"I only swing one way, ma'am. If you want more variety, you'll have to get somebody else."

"Variety? What do you mean? I give you the picture, you do the job."

"Ma'am, you must be looking for a hit man. I provide other services."

"Oh," said Lucy, color rising to her cheeks. "I'm not interested in *that*, but thanks for calling."

She put the receiver back on the hook and stood looking at it as if it would suddenly leap off the wall and attack her. Then, holding her sides with both hands, she slid onto the floor, sputtering with laughter.

Pulling herself together, she checked the clock. Her conversation with Man for Hire had taken only a few minutes; it would be at least twenty-five minutes before the next call. What was his name? She couldn't remember. In fact, it seemed eons ago, almost another lifetime, that she and Barney had sat together at the kitchen table answering the ads in *Modern Mercenary*.

At exactly ten o'clock, the phone rang. Lucy took a deep breath, and while she waited for the second ring she rehearsed what she planned to say. She picked up the receiver and said, "Hello."

"Lucy, this is Dave Davidson. I didn't wake you up, did I?" As minister, Dave knew that a lot of the women in the parish who worked the night phones at Country Cousins took naps at odd times during the day.

"No, Dave, I'm up and about. But I am expecting an important call. Could I call you back later?"

"This will only take a minute." Dave spoke in quiet, measured tones. "Can you host the coffee hour on March twentieth?"

Lucy sighed. "I guess so."

"Good. I'll put you down. You'll get a reminder the week before." His voice was very sincere as he added, "Thank you. Go in peace."

"Thank you," said Lucy, wondering how it was that whenever Dave Davidson asked her to do a favor, she ended up thanking him. She had no sooner replaced the receiver than it rang again. She snatched it up, reminded herself to calm down, and said cautiously, "Hello."

"Pest Control here."

"Thank you for calling. I have a job and I wonder if you'd be interested."

"Pest control's my business, ma'am," said the voice, chuckling.

"Well, the pest I want removed is my husband," said Lucy.

"It usually is." The voice sounded resigned. "It's sad, really. Marriage isn't what it used to be."

"I'm afraid I don't have any alternative. Divorce is out of the question."

"Of course. A direct route to poverty."

"Absolutely," Lucy agreed. "My husband has quite a lot of life insurance."

"How nice. You'll be able to maintain your current lifestyle. It's really a shame to spend all that money on hiring a professional when you could do it yourself."

"I haven't the faintest idea about how to kill someone," Lucy said indignantly. "That's why I want to hire you."

"There are definite advantages to doing it yourself," the voice informed her, sounding like a friendly hardware salesman. "Wives have so many opportunities; the average home is full of dangers that can be fatal to the unsuspecting husband."

"Really?" Lucy was incredulous.

"Absolutely. A slip in the bathtub, a short circuit in the hair dryer, cyanide in the Tylenol, there's even the bad mushroom, although that is a bit old-fashioned. If you would just give it some thought, I'm sure you could come up with a surefire method. After all, nobody knows him better than you."

"Is this what you advise all your clients?" demanded Lucy.

"Well," the voice admitted, "you're actually my first client."

"Then you aren't the man I'm looking for," said Lucy. "I'm looking for someone with experience."

"I understand," the voice said mournfully.

Lucy replaced the receiver, feeling a bit like Alice in Wonderland. Had she really had this conversation? "Curiouser and curiouser," she muttered to herself as she opened the undersink cabinet and got to work.

When the phone rang at ten-thirty, Lucy was sitting at the kitchen table, relaxing with a cup of coffee and a piece of toasted raisin bread.

"This is Bad Guy," announced the voice. "Have you been a naughty girl?"

"No, but I'm thinking of doing something very naughty," she said in a playful tone. "Are you interested?" This was sort of fun.

"I'm always interested when little girls are naughty," affirmed the voice. "I bring my own paddles, whips, and chains."

Lucy slammed the receiver on the hook and stood leaning on the counter, afraid her legs wouldn't support her. This was too much. And the worst part was that she couldn't tell anybody about it. Sue would love this. Lucy just couldn't believe these things really went on. Did they? Was it all make-believe? Did grown-ups really do this stuff? What was the world coming to? She wondered if she would ever be able to look at people in quite the same way.

When eleven o'clock came and went and the phone didn't ring, Lucy was relieved. Although the house was cleaner than it had been in months, every surface gleaming and twinkling in the bright winter sunlight, she knew it was largely an illusion. Decades' worth of dust was packed into every crack and seam, impossible even for the vacuum to suck out. She washed her hands and face, combed her hair, and carefully applied lipstick and eyeliner. Her face in the mirror looked the same as it had yesterday, but she felt different somehow. She remembered hearing as a teenager that once you lost your virginity it showed in your face. When she had finally gone all the way with an earnest second-string soccer player during freshman year of college, she was both relieved and disappointed that she couldn't see any change in her features. Grabbing her bag and keys, she decided to take Sara out for lunch at Jake's Donut Shop. It would be a treat for Sara, and she wanted to get away from the telephone for a while.

The next morning the phone rang promptly at nine-thirty. No matter what she might think of the characters who advertised their services in *Modern Mercenary*, Lucy had to admit they were certainly punctual. They must consult their field watches frequently, she thought.

"This is Combat Veteran, answering your note," said the voice in the tone of one reporting for duty. "I am ready to go into action anytime, anywhere in the world. Asia, Africa, Latin America, are all no problem for me."

"That's certainly good to know," Lucy said, impressed. "This job is in Maine."

"Maine! You must be crazy, lady. Maine in the winter! Poor tactics, extremely poor. Don't you know what happened to Napoleon in Russia?"

Lucy smiled as she replaced the receiver and pulled on a pair of rubber gloves. She reached for the oven cleaner and got to work. Half an hour later she was closing the door on a spotless oven when the phone rang. The voice on the other end was warm and reassuring.

"This is Cool Professional, answering your letter."

"Terrific," said Lucy. "I'm looking for someone to kill my husband."

"I'll want fifty thousand dollars. Twenty-five up front, and twenty-five afterward. Cash. I don't wait for insurance payoffs. Send me his name and address, a picture, and his schedule."

"As simple as that?"

"Absolutely. Perhaps you'd like to think about it for a while?" he asked courteously. "Maybe you can work something out."

"No, I've made up my mind."

"Fine."

"Just a minute," said Lucy. "Would you answer just one question for me? Have you ever killed anybody in Tinker's Cove, Maine?"

"I've never even heard of Tinker's Cove," said the voice.

Lucy believed him. Just because he was a killer didn't mean he was a liar, too.

20

#3167 Originally designed for runners' use in the winter months, these snow boots are lightweight and practical for everyday use. Uppers constructed of polyester fabric are breathable, warm, and guaranteed waterproof. Vibram soles provide excellent traction on ice and snow. Whole sizes only. Men's and women's, $69.95.

As she looked around the house, Lucy realized there was nothing left to do. Four days of steady work, fueled no doubt by postholiday letdown and premenstrual hormones, had wrought a miracle. Call *Country Homes* magazine, she thought to herself, send photographers immediately. This will probably never happen again. As she wandered from room to room, admiring the handsome antiques she and Bill had collected over the years, the afternoon stretched emptily ahead of her. Sara had a play date at a friend's house and wouldn't be coming home. Lucy climbed upstairs to change out of her grubby cleaning clothes, thinking perhaps she would spend the afternoon checking out the after-holiday sales in Portland, and noticed the bags of outgrown clothes piled on the landing.

There were some nice things in those bags: warm footed pajamas, cozy sweat suits, winter jackets, and even a pair of hardly worn snow boots bought late last winter that Sara couldn't cram her feet into this year. Lucy hated just to toss those things in a Salvation Army bin; she tried to think of someone she knew who could use them. Unfortunately none of her friends had girls younger than Sara, and her playmates all wore clothes larger than the things in the bags. Then she remembered Lisa Young's little girl. Surely she could use those clothes. Her thoughts were interrupted by Bill's voice.

"Lucy, are you home?"

"What are you doing home this time of day?" she asked, bounding down the stairs.

"I'm looking for some lunch, woman. Where's Sara?"

"At Caroline's."

"You're alone? There are no kids?" Bill was like a bird dog catching scent of a hot trail.

"That's right," Lucy admitted.

"Thank you, God," he said, reaching for her.

"Sorry, Romeo. It's the first day of my period."

"Why do you have to sound so pleased about it?" complained Bill, dropping his arms. "What's for lunch?"

"Turkey soup—homemade." Lucy hauled a big enamel pot out of the refrigerator. "And tuna fish sandwiches."

"I guess you're not such a bad wife after all," Bill conceded. "So what're you going to do this afternoon? Curl up on the couch with the kittens and a mystery?"

"I thought I'd drop off those outgrown clothes down Bump's River Road."

"Bump's River Road? I don't want you going down there," said Bill.

"I've already been down there," Lucy said. "That's where I got the kittens." She picked up Mac, who had climbed up her pant leg following the tuna fumes, and scratched his head.

"Well, don't go there anymore. A lot of weird people live down there."

"They're not weird. They're just poor," Lucy said reasonably. "Look how well the kittens turned out."

"Those people live that way because they want to, Lucy. Nothing's stopping them from working like the rest of us. Now listen to me," he said, using his authoritarian father voice, "don't go down there. Understand?"

"Yes, Daddy," said Lucy, clearing the table. As she stood at the sink rinsing off the lunch dishes and putting them in the dishwasher, she watched Bill climb into his truck and drive off. She hated it when he treated her like a child. She *was* a woman, all grown up, the mother of three children. She managed all their money, she dealt with teachers and doctors. She was capable of making decisions for herself, thank you. Besides, she kept remembering that dark-haired little girl in her torn shirt. She was just the right size for Sara's outgrown things.

Lucy loaded the bags into the Subaru and started the engine. She'd be back in plenty of time to make supper.

It was a beautiful day for a drive. The trunks of the trees lining the road were almost black and contrasted sharply with the light dusting of snow that lay on the ground. Thanks to the bright sun and the mild temperature, the snow on the road had melted. Lucy whizzed by in her little station wagon, humming along with the radio and enjoying driving all by herself for a change. She passed farms with snow-covered fields, the old farmhouses with attached barns far outnumbering the new houses on the road. As she drove farther from Tinker's Cove the farms thinned out and the road was lined with thick woods on either side.

The turnoff for Bump's River Road was just past an old store and gas station. This was a genuine country store that had made no attempt to pretty itself up for the tourists; the faded signs on the outside advertised cut plug tobacco and Nehi soda, but were overlaid with newer signs for the state lottery. A teenaged boy stood in the doorway, his long hair hanging down either side of his face and his snowmobile suit unzipped to the waist, revealing his skinny chest. He watched as she turned off the state road.

The day she had gotten the kittens she had been in a hurry, intent on following the directions she had been given, and she had not really paid attention to the scenery. Today as she passed the worn-out, shabby homes surrounded by junk-filled yards, she was horrified. Up close, in the unblinking winter sunlight, the houses looked flimsy and unsubstantial. How would these people survive the cold winter? When she had lived in the city she had grown used to seeing homeless people outside the grocery store and the bank, and there were neighborhoods she passed all the time on the train that she'd never visit. In the city she had always been aware of poor people, but since she'd moved to Tinker's Cove she'd assumed that poverty was a city problem. In the country, unless you went looking, you weren't likely to encounter real poverty.

Pulling up in front of Lisa Young's place, she smiled at the little girl sitting on the step, playing with a Barbie doll. She was absorbed in make-believe, stroking the doll's bright yellow hair and talking to it in a high-pitched sing-song voice. She didn't look up until Lucy spoke to her.

"Hi there. Is your mom home?"

The little girl disappeared inside and soon Lisa appeared at the door, wearing the same defensive expression Lucy remembered from her earlier visit.

"Do you remember me? I took the kittens before Christmas."

"Sure." Lisa stood in the doorway, the little girl clinging to her side.

"Well, I wanted to thank you. My kids really love the kittens, but that's not why I'm here," explained Lucy. "I cleaned out my daughters' closets, and I've got a lot of outgrown clothes that I think will fit your daughter. What's her name?"

"Crystal," said Lisa, still expressionless.

"I really think these will fit Crystal. Would you like to see?"

"Sure." Lisa shrugged and grudgingly followed Lucy to the car. Lucy put down the tailgate and began spreading out the garments, feeling like a saleslady as she pointed out the virtues of each item.

"This is really warm, isn't it cute?" she said, holding up an appliquéd bathrobe. "And this sweater used to be Elizabeth's favorite. She cried when it got too small." Lucy shook her head, neatly folding the sweater and replacing it in the bag.

"How much do you want?" asked Lisa.

"Nothing." Lucy was shocked. "I usually give things like this to a friend, but none of my friends have a little girl the right size. Couldn't Crystal use these?"

Lucy smiled at Crystal, who was fingering a bottle-green velvet dress with a lace collar and pearl buttons.

"Okay," said Lisa, picking up the bags. "Thank you kindly."

"You're very welcome. Can I help you carry them?"

"I can manage," said Lisa. Lucy watched her as she stepped up onto the sloping porch and went into the little cabin, closing the door firmly behind her.

Lucy turned and climbed back into the car. Do people know about this? she wondered as she turned the key and drove slowly down the muddy track. These people might as well be living in the nineteenth century, she thought, noticing that most of the houses had little outhouses behind them. How would Crystal adjust to school? How would she cope with flush toilets, bell schedules, and computers?

Deep in thought, Lucy hadn't been paying close attention to the road. She felt her car losing traction and switched to four-wheel drive, but it was too late. She'd managed to sink all four tires in the slushy mud. She opened the car door and scouted for something to put under the tires to give her some traction. She saw a yard just a bit up the road that was filled with junk. She picked her way carefully along the muddy road, glad that she'd worn her waterproof boots.

There must be something here I can use, she thought, looking about for a few boards or pieces of plywood; even a flattened cardboard box would do. She glanced at the house that was in the center of this junkyard, but no one seemed to be home. She picked her way around a broken washing machine, past bits and pieces of automobiles and lots and lots of tires, and finally found a pile of old asphalt shingles. She was bent over, picking up a generous handful, when she heard a low growl. Turning around, she saw a large, shaggy brown dog coming toward her at top speed, teeth bared and ears flat.

She dropped the shingles, scrambled up a pile of building debris, and, reaching for the branch of a big old pine tree, pulled herself to safety with just seconds to spare. Panting from fright and exertion, she wrapped her arms around the trunk of the tree and rested her forehead against it. She was perhaps seven or eight feet from the ground. The dog had climbed up the pile of debris and was standing on his hind legs, barking frantically at her and snapping his teeth at her feet. She was safe enough since he couldn't climb the tree, but she sure couldn't go anywhere.

After a while the dog stopped barking and jumping. Instead, he stood on all fours, eyeing her patiently, prepared to wait. I've played this game before, he seemed to be saying to her. Every now and then he'd bark sharply, making her jump, and then he'd resume his patient wait. Lucy shouted for help, and the dog again began barking frantically and jumping up, nipping at her feet. Lucy looked hopefully at the house, praying that someone was home who could help her. Miraculously, the door opened and a large, fat man in overalls scrambled out holding a shotgun.

"Don't shoot!" Lucy shouted. "The dog's got me stuck in this tree."

She watched in horror as the man slowly and deliberately raised the gun to his shoulder and fired. Instinctively she crouched as the shot rang out. She saw the dog's legs go out from under him as he collapsed on the junk heap, whimpered once, and went still.

Perhaps the dog belonged to someone else, Lucy thought as she jumped down from the tree. Maybe it was a nuisance dog he'd been looking for an excuse to shoot. She advanced toward the man, smiling. He had smooth round cheeks and blue eyes and smiled back at her. Then he raised the shotgun to his shoulder. Lucy ducked behind a big old steel desk just as he fired off the second round.

Lucy peeked out from behind the desk, saw that he was busy reloading, and ran for more secure cover behind a big stump of elm.

"God," Lucy prayed, "don't let this be happening to me. Let me wake up, let it be a bad dream. Please. I know. Bill was right, I was wrong. Now, get me out of here." She cringed behind the stump, shaking violently as two more shots rang out. The man wasn't coming any closer, she saw. He was still standing in the same spot, reloading again. If only he'd stop smiling at her. Damn it, that smile was familiar. She just couldn't place it. Maybe he would run out of ammunition and give up. It would be getting dark soon; maybe she could creep away in the darkness. Maybe she'd die like the dog, shot by a smiling idiot.

"Harold, put that gun down," said a voice. "Harold, I mean it. This is an order. Put it down, right now."

Raising herself just enough so she could see over the stump, Lucy saw Lisa standing at the edge of the yard, pointing her finger at the man as if he were a naughty child. Obediently he dropped the gun and shambled off to the house.

"Is that all I had to do?"

"Yeah. You just gotta let him know who's boss. He shouldn't have a gun. Dunno why they let him have it. I can't believe he shot his dog. He'll be sorry when he realizes what he done. You okay?"

"I feel a little shaky," admitted Lucy. "My car's stuck."

"You can use those shingles," Lisa informed her, walking back toward her house.

"Thanks a lot, I guess," Lucy muttered, scooping up some shingles. She spread them in front of the car tires, and by accelerating very slowly and carefully in four-wheel drive, she got going again.

She felt guilty about leaving the shingles in the road, but she absolutely could not make herself climb out of the car. Maybe they'll help someone else, she thought. Keeping her foot firmly on the accelerator and willing the car forward with every ounce of energy she had, she finally made it up Bump's River Road and pulled onto the hardtop at the store.

"Al," she said, reading the tattoo on his chest, "I wonder if you'd mind answering a question for me."

She took a ten-dollar bill out of her wallet and fingered it. "There's a big old dumb guy down there, his first name's Harold. Do you know who I mean?"

"Sure, I know him," admitted the kid, his eyes on the money.

"What's his last name?"

"Higham. Harold Higham."

"Oh, really," Lucy said slowly. She knew she'd

seen that smile before. "Well, thanks for the information," she said, passing him the bill. "I think I'll take one of those small bottles of brandy behind you."

21

Lucy got back in her car and sat for a few minutes, taking small, unsteady sips of the brandy.
She was surprised to see that according to the dig-
ital clock it was only two-thirty. It seemed like an
eternity since she'd left the house for Bump's
River Road.

She turned on the radio and let the brandy do
its work, spreading warmth through her body.
Gradually her muscles relaxed and she stopped
shaking; her teeth stopped chattering; all that remained of her fear was a hard rock in her stomach.

She didn't think she would ever forget Harold

Higham's blank, smiling face as he'd raised the
shotgun and aimed at her. Who was Harold
Higham, she wondered, and what was the matter
with him? How was he related to George? They
certainly had a family resemblance, but that's
where the resemblance ended. George's desk at
Country Cousins was always neat and tidy, his
navy blue blazer and gray flannel pants freshly
pressed. She had just assumed he came from a
solid middle-class background, but now she
wasn't so sure. She screwed the cap onto the
brandy bottle and dropped it into her purse, then
put the car in gear and turned onto the state road.

As soon as she made the turn onto the highway,
the bright sunlight made her wince. Instinctively,
she pulled down the visor and groped for her sun-
glasses. She was driving right into the sun, and
the visibility was very poor. The sun reflected off
every bit of ice and smear on the windshield, and
to make matters worse, the woods lining the road
made deep shadows. She was terrified she
wouldn't see a pedestrian or bicyclist in the shadows until it was too late.

A big pickup truck loomed suddenly behind her,
tailgating so closely that she was afraid to try to
pull over to let it pass. Her nerves already raw, she
clutched the steering wheel tightly and tried to
maintain a steady forty miles an hour. Her eyes
couldn't adjust to the changes in light and shadow
as she tried to see the road ahead, keep track of
the truck behind her, and check the speedometer.

I have to do something, she decided, and cautiously tapped the brake and turned on her left

signal. To her relief the pickup backed off, giving her room to pull over to the side. The driver, a young fellow with his black lab beside him on the passenger seat, honked and waved, and Lucy shook her head.

She was stopped, she realized, right in front of Miss Tilley's antique Cape Cod house. The little white clapboard house hugged the ground, anchored by a huge central chimney. It had been built more than two hundred years ago and was designed to stay warm even in the frigid winter winds. Impulsively Lucy turned into the driveway and marched up to the door. If anyone in town would know about Harold Higham, it would be Miss Tilley.

"Lucy, how nice to see you," she said, opening wide the solid pumpkin pine door. "I was just having some tea. Won't you join me?"

Lucy glanced at her watch. If she didn't stay long, she could still be home before the school bus.

"Thank you, I will. I'm awfully sorry about dropping in on you like this," Lucy apologized. "I have a question I want to ask you."

"I'm always glad to see you, Lucy," said Miss Tilley, leading the way into the cozy living room. Despite her age she had kept her height and her ramrod-straight back. "Lucy, do you know Emily Miller?" Miss Tilley indicated a tiny figure seated on a wing chair near the fireplace.

"Oh, dear, that fire has gotten low, hasn't it?" Miss Tilley threw another log on the fire and stirred it up with the poker. "There, that's better.

Now, Emily, this is Lucy Stone. I think I may have mentioned her to you."

"Of course, Lucy Stone. It's very nice to meet you." Although she was tiny and frail, Mrs. Miller's eyes were bright. She seemed to have recovered her strength since the day of Sam's funeral.

"I really don't want to interrupt you," insisted Lucy. "I'll come back another day."

"Nonsense," said Miss Tilley in her old library voice. "Just sit down in that rocker, Lucy, and I'll freshen up the teapot."

Lucy smiled apologetically at Mrs. Miller and did as she was told. Miss Tilley always had that effect on her; she did on everybody. Lucy didn't understand how she did it. Everyone in town knew her name was Julia Ward Howe Tilley, but Lucy had never heard anyone call her Julie, or Julia, or anything except Miss Tilley.

"Julia is so forceful," Mrs. Miller said, smiling.

Lucy's eyes widened, and she smiled politely at the old woman.

"I am awfully glad you stopped in. We have tea together quite often, and it's nice to have someone new to talk with."

Miss Tilley appeared in the doorway, carrying a loaded tea tray. Lucy watched as she stepped across a minefield of small, frayed antique rugs, but the older woman never missed a step. She sat down gracefully on a straight chair and, lifting a teacup in her left hand, poured a steady stream of steaming tea from the Royal Doulton pot she held in her right hand. She was seeing a perfect demonstration of a lost art, Lucy realized, feeling that she was taking part in some ancient ritual.

"Sugar?" asked Miss Tilley.

"No, thank you."

"Cream or lemon?"

"Lemon." Lucy leaned forward to receive the teacup and saucer and settled back in her chair, holding the fragile porcelain carefully. She still felt a bit shaky and was wondering how she could break the tranquil atmosphere with her rather awkward question.

"Lucy, you said you had something you wanted to ask me," said Miss Tilley, handing a cup to Mrs. Miller.

"I do." Lucy took a sip of tea. "I was wondering about a man named Harold Higham."

"However did you hear about him?" wondered Mrs. Miller. "He's not wandering around town, is he?"

"No. I, uh, I encountered him on Bump's River Road today."

"Whatever were you doing down there, Lucy?" demanded Miss Tilley.

Wondering how she had become the questioned instead of the questioner so quickly, Lucy replied, "I was just taking some outgrown clothes to a woman I know there."

"I thought playing Lady Bountiful had gone out of style years ago," Miss Tilley observed tartly.

Mrs. Miller cackled at her old friend's comment.

"You can't just forget those people," Lucy defended herself. "There's terrible poverty down there. If I can do something to help, what's the matter with that?"

"Well, from the look of you, I'd say your charitable impulses were resisted." Mrs. Miller chuckled.

"More than resisted, I'd say," hooted Miss Tilley. "They must have put up quite a fight."

Looking down, Lucy realized that her jeans were covered with mud and the pocket of her jacket was torn. She must be a sight, she thought, color rising to her cheeks. She laughed.

"Well, I can laugh about it now, but I was pretty scared. The car got stuck in mud, a vicious dog had me treed, and then Harold Higham shot the dog and took a few shots at me."

The two ladies clicked their tongues sympathetically.

"That's why I stopped by," Lucy continued. "I was wondering about Harold Higham. Is he related to George Higham?"

"He's his brother," said Miss Tilley.

"How can that be?" Lucy demanded. "They're so different."

"George is a remarkable man," said Mrs. Miller. "He's really his own creation. He pulled himself up by the bootstraps and walked right out of Bump's River Road."

"When he was a little boy he'd come to the library after school every afternoon. He'd settle himself in a little corner of the children's room and read there until closing time. Then he'd go walking off down the road, a tiny little fellow. I don't think they lived so far out of town then."

"No," agreed Mrs. Miller. "They lived in a ramshackle old house next to the Mobil station. It's gone now. It fell down. It was an awful place, a terrible firetrap. I used to worry about them, especially in winter. Lord knows what they used for heat."

"Probably a woodstove, set right on the floor, with a nice pile of newspapers and kindling kept handy right next to it."

"I'm sure you're right. It's a wonder it didn't burn down." Mrs. Miller shook her head.

"The father was a piece of work, I can tell you that."

"He was a dreadful man," Mrs. Miller agreed. "He used to lie on the porch steps, drunk as a skunk, throwing things at people who walked by. He called them terrible names, too."

"The mother died when George was about ten or so, I think," Miss Tilley remembered. "Poor woman was probably glad to go."

"She led a terrible life, between the husband and the idiot son."

"She might not have realized how terrible it was," observed Miss Tilley. "She wasn't very bright, as I recall."

"Wasn't there something you could do?" Lucy asked. "Today it would be called child neglect, maybe even worse."

"People did try, but all they ever got for their efforts was a torrent of abuse from the father. Or worse. Just like you did today."

"How did George manage to do so well?"

"His teachers encouraged him, and I'd let him

stay at the library. Other people took an interest in him. He was always different from the rest of the Highams."

"Maybe he's not so different after all," commented Lucy. "Thanks for the tea and the information, but I've got to go. The kids will be coming home from school."

"It's just as well you're leaving, Lucy. At four o'clock, we switch to sherry," said Miss Tilley.

"You can't imagine how decadent we can be," Mrs. Miller twinkled from her chair. "Fortunately, I don't drive anymore. Tom will pick me up and take me home."

"In a wheelbarrow," snorted Miss Tilley. "Lucy," she advised, "be careful. Curiosity is a fine and wonderful thing, but it can also be dangerous. Remember Madame Curie."

"I promise," swore Lucy, smiling, "from now on I will avoid radioactive materials. 'Bye."

Lucy caught up with the big yellow school bus on Red Top Road and followed it the rest of the way home. She put out a plate of cookies and glasses of milk for Toby and Elizabeth and sat with them at the big oak table.

Elizabeth was somewhat disgruntled; her best friend had played with someone else at recess. She consoled herself with a huge number of chocolate-chip cookies and then went off to play in peace by herself before Sara came home.

Toby only nibbled at his cookies, and Lucy instinctively asked him what was the matter.

"The Pinewood Derby is Sunday, Mom, and I haven't even started on my car."

"Well, you better get started."

"I don't know how."

"Let's look at it together."

Toby brought the little box to the table and took out the block of wood that he had to turn into a car. Lucy turned it over in her hands.

"What style car do you want to make? Have you got any ideas?"

"I want it to look like a Corvette."

Lucy smiled. "That's pretty ambitious. How about making some sketches. Then Daddy can help you cut it out tonight."

She ruffled his hair as he bent over the table, the pencil gripped tightly in his chubby hand. She smiled to see him concentrate so hard on his drawing, then went upstairs to change her clothes. It was time to get ready for work.

22

*#5999   Remington .44-caliber revolver. Features
a swing-out speed cylinder, double action with
checkered hammer. Fixed-blade front sight with
adjustable rear sight. Hammer block safety.
Molded checkered woodgrain grip. Complete with
molded carrying case. $134.95.*

Lucy stared at the blank computer screen in
front of her and hit the return key. The command
bar on the top of the screen lit up, and she read,
"Good evening, Lucy. Your rep number is 400L.
Your total sales for tonight: $14.99."

"I hate it when it's slow," she announced to no
one in particular.

"Me too," agreed Ruthie. "It's always slow after
Christmas, but I've never seen it this slow."

"It's depressing with everyone gone, but I can
see why they made the layoffs," admitted Lucy.

"I guess," Ruthie agreed. "I've been looking for another job."

"Really? Doing what?"

"Anything. I saw an ad for a ward secretary at the hospital in Portland, and I put my name in for customer service rep at K mart. There's not much out there, but anything's better than this."

"I hope you find something, but I'll really miss you," said Lucy, feeling bereft. "I miss the old gang."

Lucy's light went on, and she answered with the usual, "Country Cousins, may I help you?"

The voice that answered was clipped and very British. It was the expedition leader of a group planning to map the Andes.

"Never been done, up till now. Done properly, that is," explained the voice, which went on to order nine sets of polar underwear, nine Arctic Tundra parkas, nine pairs of Arctic Tundra pants, nine pairs of Glove-Mitts, and nine pairs of Sure-Tread boots, "guaranteed under all weather conditions."

"Do you need any camping gear?" asked Lucy.

"I'm afraid we do," complained the voice. "Lost an awful lot of stuff to a yeti in the Himalayas last spring."

"Really? I thought they were mythical."

"It's difficult to be certain," said the voice. "There's not much oxygen up there; men behave strangely in extreme circumstances."

"I suppose they do," agreed Lucy. "Now, what do you need?"

She placed orders for nine down-filled mummy bags (guaranteed to maintain body temperature to

–20 degrees), five two-man mountain tents, five flame-glo camp stoves, and a case of pressurized fuel canisters.

"Anything else? Socks, for example?"

"Good show," said the voice. "You can never have too many socks on an expedition."

"That has been my experience," said Lucy, thinking of last summer's camping trip to Mount Desert Island.

"I'll take thirty-six pairs of your very best socks."

Lucy smiled as she typed in the order—the socks alone, she figured, would come to nearly three hundred dollars.

"Do you want a total?" Lucy asked.

"Not really. We'll just let the Royal Geographical Society worry about that," confided the voice. "How soon can I expect the shipment? We're scheduled to leave on February first."

Lucy worked out the details for the geographer and smiled as he rang off with a very British, "Cheerio."

"Wow," said Ruthie as Lucy hit the return button and saw her total was now nearly ten thousand dollars.

"Boy, that was something that doesn't happen every day. That man was outfitting a nine-man mountain-climbing expedition. I think I'll call Ted Stillings. Maybe he'll put it in the paper."

"Might as well," agreed Ruthie. "There's nothing else going on."

Lucy stood up and stretched, dug her change purse out of her bag, and headed for the break

room, where the pay phone was located. She got a
diet Coke from the machine and dialed Ted's
number.

"Ted, Lucy Stone here at Country Cousins. I
think I've got a scoop for you." She gave him the
details of the order, and he promised to write it up
for the paper.

"That's a cute story, Lucy," he said. "Thanks."

"Pam told me you've been following Barney's accident. Do they know any more?" asked Lucy.

"Only that something caused the car to go right
through the guardrail. Fortunately, it got caught in
some trees. If he'd been a little farther along, it
would have gone right into the water."

"Do the police know what caused him to go
over?"

"There were tire marks showing that he
swerved. Something made him swerve, but they
don't know what. If he doesn't come to, they may
never know."

"What about the crime lab?" questioned Lucy.

"They did send stuff to be analyzed. They won't
have the results for a couple of weeks, anyway.
Hey, don't you read the paper?" demanded Ted.

"I do when I have the time," Lucy said guiltily.
"Which reminds me, I'd better get back to work."

She hung up and, walking out to the hallway,
stood reading the bulletin board and finishing her
soda. There was a strict policy forbidding liquids
near the computers, and she didn't want to risk
angering George.

Where was George tonight? she wondered. She
hadn't seen him at all, which was unusual. In fact,

peering down the dark tunnel of hallway that led to the executive offices, she didn't think any of the managers were in the building tonight.

Lucy took a last swig of soda and walked slowly down the hallway. All the offices were dark. She stood for a minute outside George's door, then impulsively reached for the knob.

It turned, and immediately she snatched her hand away and jumped back. She hadn't expected the door to be unlocked. She stood in the hallway for a minute, then slipped into the office, closing and locking the door behind her. She flipped on the wall switch and stood for a moment blinking in the brightness. Then she went over to the window and pulled down the shade.

Quickly she worked her way around the small room. She pulled out file drawers and felt behind the files; she peered into a decorative vase. She even checked the wastebasket. She couldn't have said what she was looking for, but when she opened the desk drawer and saw a black revolver, she was sure she'd found it.

She glanced around quickly to make sure she hadn't disturbed anything, switched off the light, and slipped out into the hallway. Her heart was pounding as she walked back to her desk. Whatever had possessed her to do such a thing? What if she'd been caught? What could she have said?

Sitting down at her desk, she realized how foolish she'd been. She jumped when Ruthie asked her if Ted had liked the story.

"I think so. We talked for quite a while; I was

asking about Barney. Did I miss anything?" Lucy hoped her nervousness didn't show.

"Mrs. Murgatroyd in Sioux Falls is not happy with the Dipsy-Tipsy bird feeder her son gave her for Christmas."

"No?" asked Lucy. "Why not?"

"The squirrels still get the bird seed," Ruthie told her. "She wants to return it for a refund."

"And what did you tell her?" asked Lucy.

"Just pack it in the original carton, if possible, and include the original invoice, please," recited Ruthie. "We will be happy to refund the entire purchase price. At Country Cousins, we're not happy unless you are."

"Very good," said Lucy. "What time is it?"

"Almost nine."

"Only nine?" Lucy was incredulous.

"Sorry. Want to balance my checkbook for me?"

"No. I guess I'll make up my grocery list."

Lucy thought her shift would never end. By the time the clock buzzed at one A.M. she was exhausted, twice as tired as she would have been if she'd been busy.

As she drove home along the dark, lonely roads, she kept thinking of Barney, driving along a similar country road on Christmas night. Had a shot suddenly exploded into the darkness, causing him to jump reflexively and swerve right off the road, through the black emptiness and into the trees? Had George fired that shot?

Lucy pulled the car up as close to the house as she could and ran straight into the kitchen without pausing to look, as she usually did, at the night sky.

Reaching the safety of the kitchen, she leaned against the door for a moment, panting, and then turned the lock.

Tiptoeing upstairs, she checked to make sure the kids were safely asleep. Reassured, she went back downstairs and heated some milk for herself. She knew she'd have a hard time getting to sleep.

As she sat at the kitchen table, sipping her hot milk and whiskey, Lucy tried to relax. But no matter how hard she tried, she couldn't control her thoughts. She kept thinking of the ugly black gun in George's drawer, and poor Barney, his car spinning out of control and plummeting through the darkness to the rocks below.

23

#4263   Handmade by a native Maine craftsman, this earthenware jam pot is decorated with a charming blueberry design. Complete with wooden spoon. $18.

In Maine the winter sun is very bright, and on Friday morning it poured through the kitchen windows, turning the oak table into a golden pool. The three children were sitting with their backs to the window; the morning sun seemed to give them halos. Lucy was not impressed.

"Eat your oatmeal," she advised them.

Bill bounced into the room, humming a little tune, and poured himself a cup of coffee. He sat down at the table and took a spoonful of sugar, spilling some on the table.

"Do you know you always do that? Whenever you

fix your coffee, you spill a little sugar. I'm always wiping up after you," Lucy said meanly.

"Gee, I didn't realize. I'm sorry," said Bill, raising an eyebrow and reaching for a corn muffin. He broke the muffin open with a knife, scattering crumbs on the table as he buttered it liberally. Then he compounded the mess by dropping a large blob of marmalade on the table.

"Look what you're doing!" said Lucy. "Haven't you ever heard of plates!" She picked up the muffin and plopped it on a plate, then carefully wiped off Bill's patch of table. "I have to do everything," she complained. "I work until one in the morning and then nobody helps. You just make messes and leave them for me to clean up."

"You're right," placated Bill. "I just wasn't thinking. We'll all try harder to be nice to Mommy, won't we, guys?"

The children nodded solemnly. They were wisely keeping silent this morning.

"Tell you what, Lucy. I'll leave a little late and drop Sara off at preschool for you. How's that?"

"It's no good," Lucy grumbled. "I have to go out anyway."

"Oh? I was thinking you might like to have a second cup of coffee and some time to yourself. Maybe read the paper? Have a relaxing bath? Take some Midol?"

"I have to take Marge to the hospital."

"Oh," said Bill in the tone of one who sees light dawning.

"Don't say it," Lucy warned. "You think I'm just irritable because I hate going to the hospital. That might be true, but you have to admit you're awfully messy."

"I know," admitted Bill. "But you usually don't mind."

"I do mind. You're going to have to try harder. I can't work and do all the housework, too."

"Of course not," Bill agreed. "I solemnly swear I will change my ways from now on. I will faithfully strive henceforward to be neat and clean, especially at certain times of the month." Then he added, "You don't have to see him, you know."

"I can't just drop Marge off and go shopping or something." Lucy was horrified.

"You could. You hate tubes and things, you know you do."

"Well, I'll just have to be brave. He's a friend."

"Marge would understand."

"I'd hate myself."

Bill nodded and picked up his plate and mug. He carried them over to the sink and rinsed them. Then he placed them carefully in the dishwasher.

"Do I pass inspection, Sergeant?"

Lucy laughed. "Get out of here."

An hour later she was waiting in her car outside Marge Culpepper's house. The engine was running, the radio was playing, and she was tapping the steering wheel nervously.

Marge climbed in beside her, squeezing her large self onto the small bucket seat.

"You can slide the seat back—it will give you more room."

"You can't be serious about this seat belt, Lucy. Nobody has a waist this small."

"Toby does." Lucy smiled. "He's a stick. How's Barney?"

"The same." Marge sighed.

"What do the doctors say?"

"Well, they say there's more brain activity. That means he could wake up pretty soon. But I don't know. He looks just the same. He's hooked up to all sorts of machines. It's been an awful long time."

"Less than two weeks," Lucy said.

"Seems like forever," said Marge. "I don't know how I'd have managed if it wasn't for Dave."

"Dave Davidson?" Lucy was surprised.

"Yeah," said Marge. "To tell the truth, I never really liked him a whole lot before. I guess I thought he was kinda cold, but he's really given me a lot of support. He drives me to the hospital, and talks with me about Barney. He even talks with the doctors for me."

"Hmm," said Lucy. "How's Eddie doing?"

"Pretty good." Marge sighed. "He spends a lot of time with his friends. I haven't brought him to the hospital. I didn't want him to see Barney like this."

"Is he all ready for the Pinewood Derby on Sunday? Did he get his car made?"

"He's been ready for a while. In fact, he and Barney finished up the car on Christmas Eve."

"He's way ahead of Toby. He's still got to paint his and put on the wheels. He wants to paint it the Cub Scout colors—blue and yellow."

Marge chuckled softly, then fell silent. Now and then Lucy tried to make conversation, but Marge didn't seem interested in chatting, so Lucy gave up. All too soon they arrived at the hospital. Together they walked through the automatic doors and down the long maze of hallways to the intensive care unit.

"Do you want some time alone with him?" asked Lucy.

"No. Actually, I'm supposed to meet Dave in a few minutes. You go on in. He always enjoyed your company. I'll be over at the chapel."

Standing alone outside the door, Lucy wondered what Marge meant. Surely she didn't think that Barney . . . that she and Barney were more than friends, did she? But Marge had always been completely straightforward, never one for double entendres, Lucy thought to herself, and pushed open the door.

Barney's room was bright with sunlight and full of flower arrangements; a young nurse was bustling around straightening the sheets and checking the indicators on the machines that flanked the bed. All of which served to distract Lucy—for a few minutes at least—from the figure lying there. When she finally did look at Barney, she was startled to see that his eyes were wide open. Unseeing, it seemed, but wide open.

"His eyes are open," said Lucy.

"That's right," said the nurse. "He opened them yesterday. He's also been moving his arms and legs."

"Is that normal?" asked Lucy.

"Oh, yes. Actually, they're signs of progress. He's coming closer to consciousness. One of these days someone will walk through the door and he'll say 'Hi' just as if he'd never been unconscious."

"Really?" asked Lucy.

"Really." The nurse smiled. "Isn't that right, Barney? There's more going on in that coconut of yours than people realize, isn't that so?" She spoke to Barney, looking directly into his eyes.

"Can he hear you?" Lucy was doubtful.

"We think so," said the nurse. "People who come out of comas tell us that there's a long period during which they can see and hear others but can't speak themselves. He's making excellent progress, and the doctors think he'll begin speaking any day now. I'm just going to put the radio on, and then I'll get out of here. If you need anything, ring the call button."

"Okay," said Lucy, taking off her coat and sitting on the orange plastic chair the hospital provided for visitors.

"So, you can hear me, Barney. At least I hope you can. Well, I don't know where to begin."

She looked cautiously at Barney's face but found his open eyes unnerving. A tube snaked out of his nose, an electrode seemed to be glued to a shaved patch on his skull, and an IV machine blinked at the head of his bed. A bag of yellow fluid hung from the bed rail; Barney had been catheterized. Lucy immediately averted her gaze, turning back to his face.

"Poor Barney, this is a hell of a mess. They say you're doing real well, though. Poor Marge is so worried about you, and Eddie, too. He's a good kid, Barney, and he really misses you.

"Oh, shit. You know all this stuff. I know you're working hard to get well as fast as you can."

Unable to sit any longer, Lucy got to her feet and paced back and forth between the window and the door. "I've been getting some phone calls lately, Barney. The mail-order murderers all called." She couldn't keep from smiling.

"Boy, was that a stupid scheme." Her face got red as she remembered the phone calls, and she looked at Barney to see if there was a response. But he seemed the same as before.

"If I'd been interested in weird sex, those guys were more than willing," she continued. "But I don't think any of them killed Sam Miller. Only one of them seemed like a real professional killer." She shrugged. "I guess it was a silly idea."

"Barney . . ." Her voice rose. "If you could just tell me what happened the night of the accident, it would be an awful big help. What made you swerve? A gunshot? A bright light? I have an idea," she said, dropping her voice and leaning closer to him.

She looked up, startled, as the door opened and a tired-looking Marge entered the room, along with Dave Davidson. The three of them stood awkwardly together in the small room.

Lucy smiled. "Hi, Dave."

He nodded but didn't speak to her, and Lucy thought briefly of Mr. Shay, the minister of the church she had attended as a child. Mr. Shay had been a round, jolly man who made everyone feel at ease. Dave Davidson was tall and thin, and he had a permanent slouch. Through years of counseling

sessions he'd developed the habit of helpful listening and rarely initiated a conversation himself.
Lucy had no doubt that this technique was useful
in helping troubled souls focus on their problems,
but it did little to smooth the course of social exchange, especially in uncomfortable situations in
places such as hospital rooms or even in the vesti-
bule after church services. Dave's attentive gaze
always reduced Lucy to profound speechlessness,
and as he himself did little but proffer his limp
white hand, Lucy routinely scooted past him after
church on Sundays.

As she stood there today she felt the familiar
urge to flee. But first she had to tell Marge the
good news.

"Marge, look! Barney has opened his eyes. The
nurse says one of these days he'll just start talking
as if nothing happened. Isn't that great?"

Marge and Dave didn't react with the joy she
had expected. In fact, they seemed to be waiting
for her to leave. Lucy was only too happy to oblige.

"I think I'll get some coffee. You can find me in
the coffee shop whenever you're ready."

"Thanks, Lucy."

"See you downstairs," Lucy said as the door
swung shut. But she couldn't help wondering why
Marge wasn't as overjoyed about Barney as she
was.

24

#1005 'Tater Chips are made from native Katahdin potatoes grown in Maine. Carefully sliced and kettle-cooked in 100% soybean oil, these chips are favorites everywhere. Three pounds in a decorative tin, $5.99.

Lucy stood for a moment looking at the door that had just been closed so firmly; then she shrugged and began walking down the corridor to the elevator.

The snack bar was bright and cheery; it was staffed by volunteers, mostly retirees, who enjoyed playing waitress one or two mornings a month. The food was delicious and reasonably priced. Lucy treated herself to an egg-salad sandwich, something she loved and rarely bothered to make. Taking her tray, she sat down at a table in the corner and ripped open the little bag of potato chips that came with her sandwich. From her table she had a clear view of the hospital lobby and as she ate, she enjoyed watching the passing parade.

She wasn't surprised when she saw Ted Stillings come into the snack bar. He checked in frequently at the hospital for the "Hospital News" column in the *Pennysaver.* Seeing her wave, he came over to her table, carrying his roast beef sandwich and chocolate shake.

"Hi, Lucy. You here to see Barney?"

"It was my turn to bring Marge." She brightened. "The doctors say he's making excellent progress."

"That's great news." His long, solemn face lit up in a big smile and he scratched his crew cut thoughtfully. "That accident of his is driving the cops crazy. They've gone over that cruiser with a microscope, but they can't find any sign of tampering or mechanical failure. They just can't believe Barney would go over the cliff there by accident, he knew the road too well."

"Black ice?"

"He would have allowed for it and known what to do. He'd gone to all the special cop driving classes. They all say he was a terrific driver." Ted leaned forward and lowered his voice. "Lucy, do you think he might have tried to kill himself?"

"No, not Barney. On Christmas night? You can't be serious!" Lucy exclaimed.

"It's a possibility," insisted Ted. "People do commit suicide, you know." He took a big bite of pickle. "It'd be a hell of a story. I could use a hot story right now."

"I thought Sam Miller's murder was a big story for you."

"It was. My original article got picked up by *The Boston Globe* and *The New York Times*." Ted offered this news shyly, much as Toby might show her a paper his teacher had marked "A."

"That's terrific! Congratulations!" Lucy was genuinely excited for Ted.

"It was great," said Ted. "I thought it would be a nice opportunity for me. I love Tinker's Cove and all, but I'm a little tired of small-town news. All those meetings. Last night I was at the school committee until midnight. They couldn't decide if they should cut the late bus or not. They debated for hours. I can't help wondering if I'd like a big-city paper more. I was hoping the Sam Miller story would develop into something." He shrugged. "But it never did. Nobody knows who killed Sam Miller, or why."

"I think I do," said Lucy. "And I think the same person tried to kill Barney." She sat back and waited to see his reaction.

Ted was skeptical. "Tell me more."

"Well, the person I'm thinking of had motive, means, and opportunity. Isn't that what a suspect has to have? My suspect has all three."

"Go on."

"This person is very ambitious. He comes from a very poor background, but he educated himself and got a good job at Country Cousins. I think he realized he'd gotten as far as he was going to go as long as Sam Miller was in charge. Appearances counted a lot with Sam—just look at his wife and his car—and he'd never let this man crack the inner circle. On the other hand, the guy I suspect is good buddies with Tom Miller. His chances are much better with Sam gone."

Ted smiled. "What about means?"

"A piece of hose? That's not hard to come by. And this man does have a gun—I checked. He could have fired a shot and startled Barney so he went over the cliff. I think the way these crimes were done, kind of at arm's length, goes along with this guy's personality."

"I'm beginning to think you might be on to something."

"And he had lots of opportunity at Country Cousins. He saw Sam all the time. And he doesn't have a family, at least not a family that would miss him if he was out Christmas night."

"You're talking about George Higham," said Ted, putting down his chocolate shake.

"You think he did it, too." Lucy was excited.

Ted shook his head. "George was one of the first suspects. The police investigated him thoroughly. They decided he couldn't have done it."

"Why?" Lucy demanded.

"I forget exactly," said Ted. "I think he was someplace else and could prove it."

"That doesn't prove a thing," insisted Lucy. "He probably arranged an alibi. I'm surprised Horowitz fell for it."

"Horowitz is a pro," Ted reminded her. "He knows what he's doing."

"If I could find some link between George and Barney, if I could show that Barney was so dangerous to George that he had to kill him, they'd have to investigate George again, wouldn't they?"

"Hang on a minute, Mrs. Peel. This is real life. You have a husband and kids. If he did kill Sam and tried to kill Barney, he's very dangerous. You'd better mind your own business."

"You sound just like Bill."

Ted chuckled. "It goes with the territory. The worst thing about getting older is that I sound just like my father. It hit me one day. I was telling Adam to take out the garbage and I suddenly realized I'd had the exact same conversation—from the other side—thirty years ago." He stood and picked up his tray. "I've gotta go. Paper goes to press this afternoon and I wouldn't want to leave out Mrs. Reilly's gall bladder operation."

"Last week, *The Times* . . ." sympathized Lucy.

"This week the hospital news," Ted finished for her. "Don't remind me." He paused. "You know, Lucy, I think I will stop by the barracks and have a word with Horowitz. It might be worth taking another look at George."

"Really?" Lucy brightened.

"You never know. If you're right, it'd be a hell of a story. Say hi to Bill for me."

Lucy watched Ted cross the lobby and disappear through the doors. A few minutes later Dave Davidson appeared, alone. Lucy's eyes followed him as he paused for a moment and felt his hair with tentative fingers. Other people ran their hands through their hair, they tossed their heads, they tucked a lock of hair behind an ear, thought Lucy, but Dave Davidson explored his. Evidently reassured, he continued on his way to the parking lot. A few minutes later a flustered-looking Marge Culpepper appeared. Lucy waved to her and was horrified to see Marge burst into tears.

25

#5109   *Fine Irish linen handkerchiefs are appreciated by those who still value quality. With hand-crocheted lace trim and blue forget-me-not embroidery. Set of two. $10.*

"Gosh, Marge," said Lucy, taking her by the elbow and leading her to a seat in the lobby, "I don't usually have this effect on people. Loved by one and all, that's me, or at least it was before this morning."

"Oh, Lucy," moaned Marge, dissolving into a fresh torrent of tears.

Lucy patted her hand, supplied her with a clean hankie, and murmured, "There, there," until Marge's shoulders gave a little convulsive shudder and she wiped her eyes for the last time.

"I'm sorry," she said, smiling apologetically.

"It's just that I don't know what to think anymore."

"What do you mean?" asked Lucy. "Barney's getting better. All you have to do is wait and hope. You'll have him back any day now. That's what the nurse said."

"But Dave says it's not right to let him suffer."

"What?"

"Dave says if Barney had made a living will, he wouldn't have to go through this. He says it's inhumane. No one should be hooked up to machines, to suffer endlessly, when there's no hope."

"Maybe he's right when there's no hope. But there's plenty of room for hope in Barney's case," Lucy said with what she hoped was cheerful encouragement.

"Dave says there isn't. He's seen this before, he says. It's just a cruel hoax that the doctors and hospitals play on families so they can collect weeks and weeks' worth of medical insurance."

"Dave said that? When?" questioned Lucy.

"All the time," Marge wailed. "He's been wonderful to me. I don't know what I would have done without him. He's spent so much time with me and Barney. But now he says it's time to say goodbye."

"He's going away?" Lucy was puzzled.

"Lucy, I can't talk about this here." She indicated the busy lobby. "Let's talk in the car."

Back in the car, heading for Tinker's Cove, Marge sat quietly and chewed her lip. Lucy was determined to get her talking again. She was sure

Marge had discovered the key to Barney's accident.

"Marge, what did Barney do before the accident? Did he call anyone or go anywhere? Do you remember anything that would help?"

"No," Marge remembered. "It was Christmas. We opened presents, we ate turkey. That's all. It was just a regular family Christmas." Marge's voice began to tremble, so Lucy changed the subject.

"But Dave's been real helpful?" Lucy looked over her shoulder, checked the mirrors, and accelerated onto the highway.

"He's been real nice, and I feel like I owe him a lot. Whenever I turn around he's there, ready to help me. He says he'll help me do it."

"Do what?" Lucy asked.

Marge looked around her. She took a deep breath and lowered her voice. "He says that I must summon all my courage and—" She stopped, staring down at her hands in her lap.

"And what?" Lucy asked impatiently.

"And pull the plug," whispered Marge.

"He wants you to pull the plug on Barney?" Lucy couldn't believe it. She braked and pulled the car off the road, bouncing on the rough surface. As soon as the car stopped, she turned and faced Marge. "He wants you to pull the plug on Barney?" she demanded.

"He says it's the only thing to do. That Barney is suffering. That his spirit wants to be free. That people in his condition want to die. They're not afraid. They see a long dark tunnel with a light at the other end. A warm radiant light of shining peace. Barney wants to get there more than anything, and we're holding him back. He says I must let him go. I must set him free."

Marge's voice droned on. This was a lesson she had heard so often, she knew it by heart. That she didn't accept it as true was clear from her tone, but she was also obviously afraid of disobeying her teacher.

"Nonsense, Marge. Barney's not your pet pigeon. He's a man who loves you and Eddie and wants to get back to you as soon as he can. He's coming back, Marge. I'm not kidding. I saw his legs twitch like crazy when the radio said the Celtics lost at the Garden last night."

Marge laughed weakly. "Oh, Lucy, you do have a knack for making people feel better. I'm so glad you were here, or I might have done something terrible."

"I don't think so," said Lucy.

"Oh, yes. I was really weakening. I almost did it today."

"Well," Lucy said, "you might have unhooked something, but it wouldn't have killed Barney. Those machines are just monitors. He's breathing on his own. I guess Dave didn't realize that."

"You mean—even if I had pulled the plug, it wouldn't have mattered?" asked Marge.

"Well, it might have set off some alarms, but it wouldn't have killed him," Lucy reassured her. "My father was on a life-support machine, so I know. Now, we've got to get back home. I'm going to have to pay extra at Sara's preschool as it is."

She paused, choosing her next words carefully. "Marge, if I were you, I'd try to avoid Dave for a few days. He's probably sincere and all, but Barney's getting better. Believe me."

"I don't know who to believe anymore. It's been so long, Lucy. I just want Barney back. I miss him so much."

Lucy glanced anxiously at Marge but was relieved to see she wasn't crying, just sitting quietly. "So do I. We'll really miss him at the Pinewood Derby. Last year he did such a good job as announcer."

"He really hammed it up, didn't he?" Marge recalled, smiling.

"The boys loved it. He made it sound just like a real car race. What's Eddie's car like?"

"It's pretty sharp. Bright red, with a black bumper. Some idea of his. Last year his car broke and he didn't get to finish. He thinks the bumper will help."

"That is a good idea. What did he use? Foam?"

"No, a little strip of rubber. Barney got it from Dave's wife, Carol. He remembered she used some on that sculpture she put in the front yard."

Lucy laughed. "That thing is ugly, isn't it?"

"Sure is. And she gets a lot of money for those things," said Marge.

"When they sell," observed Lucy. "Who would buy one?"

"Marcia Miller did," Marge said. "Dave said she's a real fan of her work, and got her placed in a gallery in Boston. I guess they're friends."

Lucy pulled up in front of Marge's house and

waited patiently as Marge hauled herself out of the little car.

"Thanks, Lucy. Thanks for everything."

Lucy gave her a cheery good-bye wave, then checked her watch and sighed. It was already one-thirty, and the meter was running over at Kiddie Kollege. She shifted the car into gear and turned onto Main Street, the most direct route to the pre-school. As she passed the church and the rectory beside it, she glanced at the piece of black sculpture Carol had placed on the front lawn. Impulsively she pulled the car over and stopped in front of it.

The sculpture was made of automobile parts—at least Lucy assumed the odd metal forms came from automobiles. As she studied the sculpture, she could make out two human forms: a muffler and a transmission made one, a piece of twisted fender the other. The whole piece had been spray-painted black, and a length of sturdy black hose wound the two figures together. Lucy decided she'd better take a closer look at the hose.

She turned off the ignition and climbed out of the car. She slipped as she scrambled up the steep, grass-covered bank, and as she got back to her feet the sculpture loomed over her. The piece generated a sense of pain and anguish that made Lucy uneasy. She paused to read the handwritten label that had been placed at the base of the statue and then jumped back as if she'd been bitten. "Bondage of Love," it read.

Lucy leaned forward to examine the hose, reaching out and wrapping her fingers around it. It felt just as she expected it would. For now there was no doubt that she had tried to pull a piece of the exact same hose from Sam Miller's car window.

Carol worked in an old barn behind the house, and that's where Lucy went, her ankle smarting. She didn't want to go, but she had to talk to Carol. Things were beginning to add up, and she didn't like the way her thoughts were headed.

The big barn door was unlatched and yielded to her hand with a noisy scrape. She stepped into the dark and waited a moment for her eyes to adjust. She looked up toward the loft window, and there she saw Carol's limp body, swaying slightly, silhouetted by the bright afternoon sun.

26

#3335 Magnetic slate is a copy of the slates used by students in one-room schoolhouses but can be affixed to the refrigerator and used as a noteboard. A useful memory jog. $12.

"This is getting to be a bad habit, Mrs. Stone," said Lieutenant Horowitz as he sat down opposite Lucy at Marge's kitchen table. He made an odd snorting noise; he was obviously enjoying his little joke.

Lucy narrowed her eyes at him and took another swallow of the sweet tea Marge had brewed for her. After making her gruesome discovery at the rectory, Lucy had driven right back to Marge's house and called the state police. Horowitz and a team of investigators had arrived in a matter of minutes. Now the team was already at work gathering evidence at Carol's studio, and Horowitz was questioning Lucy.

"Now, Mrs. Stone, why did you stop at the rectory?" Horowitz had his notebook out and was ready to record her answer.

"Because of the hose. The hose on the sculpture. No. Wait. Because Marge told me that Dave was trying to get her to pull the plug on Barney. That didn't seem right to me, and then she said Barney got a piece of hose from Carol and I wondered if it was the same hose used to kill Sam Miller. And it was." Lucy leaned her head on her hand. She'd never felt so tired.

"Davidson wanted Mrs. Culpepper to pull the plug on Barney?" asked Horowitz.

"That's right," said Marge. "He's been after me for weeks. Keeps telling me it's cruel to keep him alive when there's no hope. I believed him, too, until Lucy told me Barney's getting better. The nurse told her. Dave had talked to the doctors for me. . . ." Marge's voice trailed off. "I thought he was helping me," she whispered.

"What about the hose, Mrs. Stone?"

Lucy snapped to attention. "The hose. I stopped to look at the sculpture, and there was some black hose on it. I wondered if it was the same hose that was used to kill Sam Miller. It was."

"So Dave Davidson killed Sam Miller?"

"I think so," Lucy said.

"And tried to kill Barney," added Marge.

"Why?" said Horowitz.

"It's all in the sculpture." Lucy sighed. "Dave was having an affair with Marcia Miller."

Horowitz and Marge exchanged a glance.

"Run that by me again," said Horowitz.

"Just look at the sculpture. It's called *Bondage of Love*," explained Lucy. "It's two figures, Dave and Marcia, in an embrace. They're bound together by the hose, by the fact that Dave killed Sam. Jealousy, hate, it's all there," Lucy said matter-of-factly. "It's a public proclamation by Carol that Dave was having an affair with Marcia Miller and killed her husband. He'll never be free of her. That's why Carol hanged herself."

"You got that out of the sculpture?" Horowitz was skeptical.

"Why else would she use all those auto parts?" asked Lucy. "Cars were Davidson's weapon of choice."

"Barney saw them together," Marge said flatly. "He didn't think there was any hanky-panky, of course. He wouldn't, with Dave being a minister and all. But he did say to me once that Marcia Miller must be a lot more religious than anyone realized because he saw her leaving the church so often on Tuesday afternoons." Her face was a study in disbelief.

"Tuesday afternoons?" exclaimed Lucy. "In the church?"

Marge nodded. Horowitz pursed his lips and made a note. Lucy stifled an ever-growing urge to laugh hysterically.

"They sure fooled me," confessed Marge. "They fooled everybody. Not an easy thing to do in a town like this."

"They didn't fool Sam," said Lucy. "If he hadn't been so smart, he'd probably still be alive."

"The problem is that all this is hearsay and rumor. I can't see that sculpture convincing a jury," observed Horowitz. "In order to get a conviction these days you've got to have everything on videotape. Whispering in your ear isn't a crime, Mrs. Culpepper."

"He's there with Barney!" remembered Marge. "I left him there at the hospital! He's alone with Barney—I've got to get back there!"

"Maybe you can get him on tape after all," said Lucy dryly.

27

#8795   Havahart trap is the humane way to dispose of nuisance animals such as skunks and raccoons. The trap confines but does not harm the animal so it can be released back to its proper environment. 100% rustproof steel construction. Small, $40; medium, $55; large, $75.

"Lucy, I'm so scared I don't think I can stand it. I'm afraid I'll pee in my pants," Marge said with a moan, clutching Lucy's hand. The two were in the backseat of a cruiser, speeding down the highway to the hospital in Portland.

"I know," agreed Lucy. "He's a killer. He killed Sam Miller, and he almost succeeded in killing Barney. I hope we're in time."

"How am I going to pretend I don't know he's guilty? I keep thinking about Carol—he doesn't even know his own wife is dead."

"Just try to forget. Make believe it's yesterday. Dave's just the minister of your church, trying to help you make a difficult decision."

"I don't think I can. My stomach's killing me. I think I have to throw up."

"Here, suck on this," said Lucy, giving her a broken candy cane she found in the bottom of her purse. "You need a little sugar." Seeing Marge so shaken and white-faced, she continued, "You've got to pull yourself together, Marge. This is the only way that they can make a case against Davidson. Barney won't be safe until he's put away."

"I know. I guess I've always been a little bit afraid of him," admitted Marge. "The minister, you know, like a teacher but with God backing him up."

"I don't think God's on his side anymore. Besides, I'll be there for you. And Horowitz, and probably half the state police. All you have to do is be yourself."

Marge took a little quivering breath and squared her shoulders as they pulled up in front of the hospital. A trooper helped them out of the car, and they hurried through the door and into the lobby. When the elevator doors opened a nurse met them and led them to the room next to Barney's, where Horowitz was waiting for them.

"Okay," he told Marge. "Everything is set. There's a video camera in the room, and a tape recorder, too. You'll be under observation at all times. My men"—he indicated two state troopers in the room—"are only a few steps away. You're absolutely safe, and so is your husband. All you have to do is make Davidson incriminate himself. He has to tell you to kill him, or he has to take some action that would kill Barney. Do you understand?"

Marge's eyes were enormous, her mouth tiny as she nodded.

"Okay. You go on in the room and wait for him. We'll have him paged."

"Good luck." Lucy smiled and patted her hand. "You can do it."

Lucy watched as Marge left the room, then reappeared on the video screen. Horowitz and the two uniformed state police officers stood behind her, also watching the screen.

"I have two men dressed as orderlies in the hall," said Horowitz. Just then, they heard the public address system call for Reverend Davidson to go to room 203, and Horowitz said, "Now we just have to wait."

Cool and self-contained as always, he stood watching the video monitor. To Lucy the scene on the screen looked like something from a daytime soap opera. There was the hospital room filled with flowers and cards. There was the bed surrounded with blinking and beeping pieces of machinery. There was the patient lying still, unconscious.

They watched as Marge settled herself on a chair next to Barney's side. They saw her take his hand in her own and stroke it gently. They heard her soft words as she greeted him. Still unconscious, he showed no reaction to her presence but lay peaceful and still, defenseless as a napping baby.

Marge looked up sharply, and suddenly Dave Davidson appeared on the screen. She stood up awkwardly as he embraced her.

Watching the screen, Lucy shivered. How could evil be so self-effacing and mild-mannered? She preferred the directness of Cool Professional to the hypocritical helpfulness of the minister. The men around her tensed. One officer was nervously fingering a walkie-talkie, and the other stood by the door with his pistol in his hand. They were ready to spring the trap.

"This is a sad business," said Davidson, withdrawing from the embrace and patting Marge mechanically on the back.

"Well . . ." Marge sighed. "His condition never changes. I'm afraid this will go on for years."

"I've seen that happen. It's a terrible thing to watch." The minister shook his head mournfully. "Now he's still robust and peaceful, but not for much longer, I'm afraid. As the weeks and months go on, he'll gradually deteriorate. You'll see him getting thinner and thinner. He'll curl up into a fetal position. His hair will become dry, his skin coarse and white. His eyes and cheeks will sink and he'll look like a corpse, but they won't let him go. The doctors, these scientists"—he spat out the word—"will keep him alive no matter how hopeless his condition. It's a living hell. You will suffer watching him, and make no mistake, he will be suffering, too. His spirit is yearning to be set free."

Even on the screen Lucy could sense the intensity and magnetism of Davidson's appeal.

"He's not afraid," crooned the minister in Marge's ear. "He wants to be released, to climb a sunbeam and join the angels."

Marge's eyes shone with faith and desire. "What must I do?" she asked.

"It won't be hard," he assured her. "All you have to do is unplug the equipment." He dismissed the battery of machinery with a wave of his hand. "Then Barney's soul will slip away. He will find the peace that passeth all understanding."

"Will you help me?" asked Marge. "Will you stay with me?"

Lucy saw a flicker of hesitation cross Davidson's face, but then he murmured, "Of course."

"Thank you," whispered Marge. "I think I'm ready. Should we do it now?"

"Yes," said Davidson, taking her hand and leading her to the outlet behind the bed. Lucy stood transfixed as she saw Dave push Marge's hand toward the plug.

"Just unplug it," Davidson whispered. "Nothing simpler."

He placed Marge's hand on the plug and wrapped her fingers around it. Covering her hand with his, he pulled. The machinery sighed, and suddenly the room was deathly quiet.

Lucy realized she was holding her breath and gasped for air. Horowitz hissed, "Go." The officer with the walkie-talkie spoke into it. "Now. Grab him."

They rushed from the room, and Lucy watched

as they reappeared on the screen. "David Davidson, I am arresting you for the attempted murder
of Barney Culpepper. You have the right to remain
silent . . ."

Lucy went to the doorway and watched as they
led Davidson, handcuffed, down the long hospital
corridor. Entering Barney's room, she saw that
Marge had already replaced the plug. She put her
arm around her shoulders and stood with her,
watching Barney's chest rise and fall.

"It doesn't seem to have done him any harm,
but I think I'll call the nurse just to be sure," said
Marge. She had just bent to ring the call button
when Barney's eyes flew open. She jumped back in
shock.

"What's going on here?" Barney demanded.

28

#3076 Surprise mugs. These white stoneware mugs have a surprise on the bottom for good little boys and girls who finish their cocoa. Specify frog or kitten. $6.50.

"Of course they were having an affair," said Emily Miller, her white head bobbing and her blue eyes twinkling over her tea cup.

Her ancient friend, Miss Tilley, nodded. "I said so all along, if you remember."

"It was certainly a surprise to me," Lucy confessed.

Once again she was having tea with the two old friends, and this time she was dressed for the occasion. She was wearing a brand-new blouse and sweater she'd bought at the Country Cousins January overstock sale. Her ankles were clamped together neatly, a linen napkin was perched on her knees, and she was using her very best manners. In fact, she felt rather like a child at an adult party, a sensation she was doing her best to overcome.

"No, I didn't know, and I don't think most other people did, either. I was sure George Higham did it," she admitted, taking a sip of tea and nearly choking on its odd, smoky flavor.

"It's Lapsang souchong, dear. Perhaps you'd like something milder?" inquired Miss Tilley.

"Oh, no, this is fine. In fact, I rather like it," Lucy insisted bravely.

The two old women exchanged a glance.

"I've always thought you had possibilities, Lucy Stone. You always chose such eclectic reading material," remembered Miss Tilley. "Now, do tell us all about that dreadful afternoon." She settled back in her chair and took a sip of tea, rolling it over her tongue and savoring it.

"I'd taken Marge to the hospital to visit Barney," Lucy began. "She told me that Dave Davidson was encouraging her to pull the plug on Barney. He kept telling her that Barney would never recover, and that the kindest thing to do would be to end it. It made me suspicious because the nurses told me Barney was getting better."

"How is he doing, Lucy?" asked Mrs. Miller.

"He's doing wonderfully. Every day he's stronger and remembers more. I will never forget how he came out of that coma. One minute he was unconscious, and the next he was wide awake, demanding to know what was going on. It was amazing."

"Of course, if the Reverend Mr. Davidson had had his way, it would have been very different," Miss Tilley added tartly. "Such a wicked man."

"I always tried to avoid him after church," confessed Lucy. "I never liked him. He made me uneasy. Of course, I never thought he was a murderer until I saw the sculpture."

"Carol's sculpture? That did surprise me," said Miss Tilley.

"The sculpture? I never did like her work, either," observed Lucy.

"No, no, dear. Not the sculpture. So original. No, the way she hanged herself. I would have expected her to react differently. I rather liked her, you see. She didn't behave the way a minister's wife is supposed to. She never went to church; she had a career of her own. I admired that. I was very disappointed to hear she'd killed herself."

"True grit," commented Mrs. Miller. "She didn't have it."

Mrs. Miller certainly had grit, thought Lucy. She would never let anyone see her grieve for her son.

Grief, like love, was private.

"Well, it must have been pretty devastating," said Lucy. "First her husband had an affair with Marcia; that would be awful for any woman. And then she figured out he'd murdered Sam, and almost murdered Barney. It would be pretty hard to take, especially if she loved him."

"Young people are so romantic," Mrs. Miller said.

"I wouldn't call this romantic," said Miss Tilley.

"Not in the true sense of the word. I would call it maudlin."

The other women nodded automatically. After forty years as a librarian no one argued with her about facts. Or definitions.

"What about the sculpture? How did it make you realize Davidson was the murderer?" asked Miss Tilley.

"The black hose. Carol had wrapped it all around the sculpture. It was the same hose Dave used on Sam's car." Lucy dropped her voice. She hated talking about Sam with his mother.

"A public declaration of his guilt?" Mrs. Miller asked a little shakily. Lucy was reminded again that this must still be hard on her.

"I think so," she said. "Barney had stumbled on the hose when he mentioned to Carol that he needed something for Eddie's car. The Cub Scouts are having the Pinewood Derby this month—you know, they race little wooden cars that they make themselves. Well, Barney was looking for some scraps of rubber to make a bumper for Eddie's car. Knowing Carol was a sculptor and apt to have bits and pieces around, he asked her if she had something he could use. When she gave him a bit of black rubber hose, he recognized it as the same hose that was used on Sam Miller's car. Barney was going to take it to the police lab the day after Christmas, but he never made it. Dave must have realized Barney had the evidence that could convict him, and decided he had to get rid of him. He parked out near the point, and when Barney came round the bend he turned on his high beams. Barney swerved right off the road."

The two women clicked their tongues. "I wonder how many of the Ten Commandments he actually broke," Miss Tilley mused. "Definitely the seventh, and the sixth, of course."

"He was covetous, and he lied," Lucy added.

"And Marcia certainly became more important than God to him. She had that effect on a lot of men, including Sam, I'm sorry to say." Mrs. Miller helped herself to another piece of banana bread.

"He did remember the Sabbath," said Miss Tilley, determined to be fair. "And I must say I never heard him swear. That's more than many Christians can claim."

Lucy and Mrs. Miller chuckled.

"I don't know what he can expect in the next life, but I hope he will be punished in this life." Mrs. Miller smoothed the napkin in her lap.

"Oh, yes. Detective Horowitz told me they have an airtight case. Carol left a detailed suicide note, and of course they videotaped him trying to convince Marge to pull the plug."

"And you saw the police arrest him?" asked Miss Tilley.

"How did he react? When he knew the game was up?" Mrs. Miller sounded serious.

"He seemed angry," Lucy reported. "He didn't say anything, but he looked furious."

"I hope he's punished," said Mrs. Miller. "I hope he doesn't get off on some sort of technicality."

"I don't think he will," said Lucy. "What about

Marcia? And your grandson? Will they come back?"

"I don't think so. She's living in Paris. She writes to me, you know. I think Tinker's Cove was a bit tame for her. I may visit them this summer."

Lucy smiled at her. The resilience of this old woman amazed her. She reached for a piece of banana bread, chewed it thoughtfully, and, sipping her tea, she observed the two old women. Miss Tilley with her large, strong features covered with a tough netting of wrinkles, her long white hair drawn up in a bun; and Mrs. Miller, with a round face just like a dried apple-head doll and her carefully curled and blued hair. In the life of Tinker's Cove they were forces to be reckoned with. As ardent conservationists they had been instrumental in creating the Tinker's Cove Conservation Trust. Miss Tilley had spearheaded the local literacy program, and she was a frequent contributor to the letters column in the *Pennysaver*. Together the two women acted as a collective conscience for the town. They were vital, strong women who were interested in the world around them.

Lucy thought of funerals she had attended where all the women of her generation were in tears, their faces bleak and uncomprehending, their knuckles white as they clutched crumpled tissues. Death was unbelievable to them, an assault on everything they worked so hard to maintain.

The older women, Lucy had noticed, never seemed as distressed. They rarely cried but sat silently through the service, gathering in small groups afterward to comfort each other. When it was time to speak with the bereaved they knew what to say, while Lucy and her friends could only babble clichés such as "Call me if there's anything I can do."

She had always admired the acceptance and assurance of these women; she had hoped that in time she would grow to be like them.

She thought of her mother. Her mother had never accepted death the way these women did. Although she was in her sixties, the death of her husband had left her as raw and hurt as if she were a young bride. Her mother had never developed the self-protective detachment so many older women grew.

Lucy wondered what life held for her and how she would cope. Would she maintain her naiveté and her vulnerability, as her mother had, or would she turn into someone as wise but as cynical as Miss Tilley?

"We've been keeping an eye on you, Lucy." Miss Tilley interrupted her thoughts.

"Yes, you seem . . . well, interesting," agreed Mrs. Miller. "You're not afraid to get involved."

"My husband wouldn't agree with you," observed Lucy. "He's always telling me to mind my own business."

"Oh, husbands," Miss Tilley said dismissively.

"I'm afraid I'd better be getting back to mine. He's watching the kids today." She stood up reluctantly and said her good-byes. But as she drove home she kept thinking of the two old women.

Pulling into the driveway, Lucy was surprised

not to see any sign of the kids. Maybe Bill had gotten a video for them, but she thought they really ought to be outside on such a nice day. As she opened the front door, she didn't hear the TV, and she was surprised when Bill met her in the kitchen.

"Where are the kids?" she asked him.

"Your friend Sue took them over to the new playground in Gardner."

"She did? Why'd she do that?"

"Well, she's your best friend, and she thought you might enjoy a little time alone with your husband."

"I don't suppose you had anything to do with that," Lucy said, smiling.

"I might have," said Bill, slipping his arms around her waist.

Lucy raised her face to his and was rewarded with a long, loving kiss.

"Oh, Bill," said Lucy. "If I let you have your way with me, will you respect me afterwards?"

"I hope not," said Bill, leading her upstairs.